LLANO RIVER VALLEY

LLANO RIVER VALLEY

•

Kent Conwell

AVALON BOOKS
NEW YORK

Published by Thomas Bouregy & Co., Inc.
160 Madison Avenue, New York, NY 10016

Library of Congress Cataloging-in-Publication Data

Conwell, Kent.
    Llano River Valley / Kent Conwell.
        p. cm.
    ISBN 978-0-8034-9931-7 (hardcover : acid-free paper)
1. Confederate States of America. Army—Officers—Fiction.
I. Title.

PS3553.O547L63   2008
813'.54—dc22   2008023400

PRINTED IN THE UNITED STATES OF AMERICA
ON ACID-FREE PAPER
BY HADDON CRAFTSMEN, BLOOMSBURG, PENNSYLVANIA

To my grandson, Mikey, and to Susan
and Mike who by now are well aware
their lives will never be the same.

And to my wife, Gayle.

Chapter One

I suppose on the nights my Kiowa brother Red Eagle and I squatted in the shadows of the teepee and listened to our father Big Horse and his blood brother Skywalker—the medicine man who was said to have the powers of prophecy—I should have paid more attention to their words.`

But I didn't. I didn't even pay much more attention in the following years when between traveling shows Professor Thornton struggled to pour what education he could into my empty head.

Skywalker always preached patience and determination to the Kiowa, and the professor lectured me on it. But the older I grew the more I found myself growing shorter on both, a combination that sure enough begged for trouble.

That ill-matched combination was the main reason I found myself leaning against the bar in the Long Branch Saloon in Dodge City, looking forward to spending every cent I had earned eating dust and fighting off Comanche on the three-month cattle drive up from South Texas. I figured a weeklong binge, drinking myself blind, would wash the dust from my throat.

For the last four years since 1864 I'd been at loose ends. A dishonorable discharge from the Confederate Army doesn't do much to bolster a jasper's self-esteem even if the discharge was based upon lies.

I had no idea why Hugh Garrett lied. All I knew was that he was as shy of the truth as a goat is of feathers. While my character witnesses at the court-martial were enough to keep me from the firing squad, they could not offset the deceit of Corporal Garrett, who was killed in a Yankee mortar attack only hours after he testified and just minutes before I got my hands on him.

In my early years with the Kiowa and later with Professor R Wellington Thornton of Thornton's Traveling Circus, I learned that money or power never lasts, but a good name comes from helping others, and as such, lasts forever. Mine had been blown higher than a sunfishing bronco when Garrett lied under oath.

And now I could do nothing about it. Funny thing about shame, whether deserved or undeserved, once it's pinned to your lapel, you view everyone differently, wondering if they've heard of your past.

That's why I moved back West, planning on a new start that never quite found a foothold.

"Cheer up cowboy. You look lonelier than a horse thief in front of a hanging judge. How about buying me a drink?"

I looked around as a painted hurdy-gurdy girl wedged in between me and another cowpoke, a cigarette dangling from her bright red lips and her eyes glazed from rotgut liquor strong enough to draw blood blisters on a rawhide boot. Her eyes flicked to the scar on my cheek and she grinned. "I'm thirsty."

The smile on my face had tightened when she looked at my scar. It was a small one, the result of a saber at Murfreesboro in early '63, but it reminded me of the war and my disgrace. I motioned to the bartender, who promptly slid two glasses of whiskey on the counter.

She sipped her whiskey and leaned forward, ready to whisper a proposal. At that moment, a hand waved at me from across the smoky room. "Hey, JC," a voice shouted. "We got room for one more in this here poker game."

I peered through the smoke. I saw a redheaded jasper and then recognized him. It was Wishbone, one of the drovers on the drive up. He picked up the handle Wishbone because his legs were so bowed you could drive a hog through them without touching either one.

Him and me had met in the Army, tore up one or two saloons together, and then ran into each other on a cattle drive three years before. Since then, I'd worked two more drives with him. He was one of the few jaspers who knew about me and my troubles.

For the next thirty minutes the five of us played a friendly game, losing a few dollars, winning a few, but generally enjoying the camaraderie of those of our own kind, anonymous cowpokes who, come the next morning, would be gone and forgotten, like lonely tumbleweeds pushed across the prairie by vagrant winds, leaving no footprints in the sand.

As the game progressed, talk turned to future plans. "Me," cackled Wishbone. "Soon as I lose all my pay, I'm heading back south, maybe stop off in Fort Worth and visit the old folks 'afore they take that stairway to heaven."

We all laughed.

"What about you, JC?"

I bet two dollars. "I figure on wandering back to South Texas and find a place to winter, then hook up on another drive next spring."

Too bad those plans exploded in my face.

We were joking about the vagaries of luck and one of the cowpokes made the idle remark, "I don't reckon I'll ever have the kind of luck that old Hugh Garrett got."

Despite the straight flush building in my hand, I froze and gaped at the cowpoke. Instinctively, I laid a finger on the scar on my cheek. "What's that you say? Garrett? Hugh Garrett?"

Wishbone looked at me in surprise.

The lanky cowpoke grinned, revealing two missing front teeth. "Yep. You know him?"

Struggling to remain calm, I shrugged. "I knew a Corporal Hugh Garrett from the Three-Seventy-Seventh Louisiana."

The cowpoke slid his John B Stetson to the back of his head, revealing a white band across his forehead and studied his cards, then raised the bet. He lifted an eyebrow. "Well, might be. This one was a butternut corporal. I don't recollect what regiment. He was from Virginia."

"Virginia?" I tried not to stutter. The Hugh Garrett who lied at my court-martial was from Virginia. Could he still be alive? I called the cowpoke's raise and casually asked, "So, what kind of luck did this hombre run into?"

While the other players called and raised, a frown wrinkled his forehead. "That's what I meant, that lucky critter. He hadn't been home in years, and one day he got hisself a letter from some carpetbagger lawyer saying he was heir to the family plantation back in Richmond."

Wishbone and I exchanged knowing looks. I did my best to suppress my excitement. "I reckon some jaspers have all the luck. When did all this take place?"

He glanced at me curiously for a moment, then shrugged, figuring I was just a nosy cowpoke. "Last week, right here at the Long Branch. He bought us all a round of drinks and caught the next train out for St. Louis." He called the raise.

I studied my cards. The dealer gave me the fifth one. Another heart but not the one I needed. Still, I had five hearts, a nice little flush.

The betting made another round. Despite my excitement, I remained silent, not wanting to make the cowpoke suspicious.

With a broad grin, he laid down his cards. "Three big kings," he boasted.

I stared at my flush, then decided to give the cowpoke the pot to keep him happy. "Beats me." Shaking my head, I added, "I reckon there's thousands of Hugh Garretts around. I shared a tent with a jasper by that name after he was busted back to corporal." The last was a lie, about sharing a tent.

The cowpoke glanced up while raking in his pot. "I bet it's the same hombre. He mentioned something like that. Some broomtail officer busted him just to cover his own keister."

Wishbone grinned at me and nodded briefly.

The next eastbound train pulled out of Dodge City three hours later at 6 A.M. Having sold my horse and saddle, I waited on the loading platform to board.

At my side, Wishbone cleared his throat. "You really reckon that mortar didn't kill that hombre?"

I ran my finger over the scar. "I've seen stranger things."

He gave me a crooked grin and stuck out his hand.

"Good luck, JC. You need anything, I'll be in Fort Worth at my folks."

With a grin of my own, I nodded. "Obliged."

The next several days seemed to drag. Although the war was three years over, repairs to the rails continued. As we moved into Kentucky and Virginia, rail travel gave way to stagecoaches and horseback for a few miles until we found another stretch of rails.

During the long days and nights, a hundred ideas of what I should do with Garrett popped into my head, but none of them held water. It was my word against his. All he had to do was deny, and if I threatened to shoot him the law would say he admitted lying just to save his own life.

Still, I had to give it a shot.

Richmond was overrun with scalawags and carpetbaggers, all swooping down like buzzards from the north during Reconstruction hoping to return to comfortable homes back up in Pennsylvania and New Jersey with Southern gold lining their pockets.

I found a livery where I managed to rent a horse and saddle for a gold eagle, an outrageous sum, but one that was the going price and had to be met. The old man who brought me my horse, a sorrel, eyed my dress and the sixgun on my hip. "You from Texas?"

"Yep." I swung into the saddle.

"Figured as much with that hogleg. Folks ain't been wearing hardware like that around here for quite a spell. Sorry about the charge. It wasn't like that when I ran this place before the war, but Yankee from Philadelphia took it over when I couldn't meet the taxes. He's doing his dadnabbed best to draw blood from every poor jasper what comes by."

With a grin, I nodded. "It's like that down in Texas too, partner."

A couple hours later, I paused at the entrance to the narrow road winding back through the forest to the Garrett plantation. Shucking my .36 caliber Colt, I checked the cylinders and caps, holstered my revolver, and deliberately left the rawhide loop off the hammer just in case I needed the gun fast. I still had no idea what I was going to do when I confronted Garrett.

Ten minutes later, the fact I had no idea what I was going to do made no difference.

Chapter Two

In the charming antebellum days of fancy cotillions and balls, I reckoned the plantation had been truly magnificent. But now, in gloomy postbellum days, thick vines covered the crumbling brick walls of the main house; black mold wrapped around the Corinthian columns; the clapboard barn had caved in on itself; once lush fields were overgrown with weeds; and the slave quarters were crumbling.

Reining up fifty yards or so before reaching the main house, I studied the decaying plantation with a sense of regret. The days of charm and grace and beauty were only memories.

There was no sign of life. A few birds played in the trees; two rabbits munched on fresh grass; and clouds of gnats, looking so much like gray balloons, swarmed above fields of weeds.

Suddenly, movement caught my eye at one corner of the mansion. My hand went to the butt of my Navy Colt then hesitated. A black face appeared, staring at me warily.

I held up my hand and rode forward, reining up about thirty feet from the withered old man. "Howdy."

The tonsured strip of hair around his skull was solid white, a sharp contrast to the color of his face and baldpate. His clothes hung in tatters on thin bones that seemed to be held together with nothing more than shriveled skin. He nodded. "Yes, suh."

"This your place?"

He shook his head. "No, suh. Not no more. Was for almost eighty years. But no more. De place, it going to de tax man."

Surveying the plantation once again, I could see in my mind's eye the gaiety that once prevailed beneath the spreading oaks and gently swaying Spanish moss. I felt a sense of loss, but certainly, not to the same extent as those who had once enjoyed such luxury.

I frowned, wondering just what had taken place to put Hugh Garrett in the Confederate Army instead of remaining here and paying a slave to take his place.

In a nonthreatening tone, I said, "I'm looking for Hugh Garrett. I understand he owns this place now."

The old slave shook his head. "No, suh. Mr. Garrett, he don't own nothing no more."

"But, he did come back."

"Yes, suh. Mr. Garrett, he come back, but when he ups and sees de taxes he owes on de place he turns hisself right around and goes back where he come from."

The lessons old Skywalker and the professor had tried to pound into my skull came flooding back. Patience and determination. I suppressed the curse boiling to come out of my lips. "And where did he go back to?"

"I don't really know what it is, suh." He pointed a bony finger toward the setting sun. "He call it Arizony Territory." He paused and muttered wistfully. "They say I be free man now. How far be Arizony? Mayhaps I goes there."

I cursed all the way back into Richmond. I'd spent a couple weeks and a good chunk of my money on the trip, and now I had to backtrack. But, I reminded myself, Garrett is alive, and I'm only a week or so behind him.

All I had to do now was find him and somehow convince him to admit he lied at my court-martial.

For the first time in four years, I felt alive.

Returning my pony, I purchased a ticket on the 10 o'clock train for Knoxville, Tennessee after which I asked around town about Garrett. Naturally, no one remembered seeing him, but I reminded myself that the one advantage I had was that Arizona Territory was sparsely populated, and someone like Garrett would head for towns like Tucson or Phoenix, or Flagstaff or even Prescott.

Just before six, I stopped in at the local tonsorial parlor for a haircut, shave, and bath. Remembering the old livery man's comment about my Colt, I rolled my gunbelt into my soogan before heading over to the Chilton House for supper. I brushed the dust off my black Stetson and straightened my leather vest.

The dining room was crowded but a smiling young woman showed me to a table by one of the front windows where I tossed my soogan on one chair and my Stetson on another. I ordered a thick steak, cooked just enough so it wouldn't walk off the plate, potatoes, cream gravy, buttered rolls, apple pie, and a bottle of Old Crow whiskey.

I was tired but I reckoned on sleeping during the train ride after I put myself around a solid supper.

Carpetbaggers might have owned the Chilton House but they certainly didn't do the cooking. The food was southern style, rich, filling, and plenty of it.

While I couldn't help noticing that my western dress was drawing curious stares from many of the more fashionably dressed diners, I shrugged off their amused glances and enjoyed my meal. I'd be out of here in forty-five minutes.

Halfway through my meal, a skinny jasper in a black suit paused at the table next to me and spoke to the diners. I paid no attention but I couldn't help noticing that waiters gathered the guests' dining ware and moved it to another table in the rear of the dining room.

Moments later the skinny jasper stopped at my table. I

guessed he was probably the headwaiter. "Excuse me, sir." He sniffed and indicated the three empty chairs at my table with a terse nod. "We are very crowded tonight. Mr. Rawlings and his entourage have arrived, and we must put two tables together. Would you mind moving to another table?"

Normally, I'm fairly well easygoing, and at the moment, I figured I might as well help out the Chilton House. I glanced at the main entrance. A rotund man in full dinner dress with a beautiful woman wearing a revealing evening gown on either side of him, stood glaring around the room with the high-handed look a stud bull gives his harem of heifers. He sure didn't look like he'd come to town riding on a mule.

Keeping my eyes on the stud bull, I asked, "Who in Sam Hill is Mr. Rawlings?"

My question startled the headwaiter. He stammered, "Why–why, Mr. Rawlings is Mr. Rawlings, the owner of the Chilton House and several other businesses in Richmond."

My eyes narrowed. "Yankee?"

Sputtering, the headwaiter coughed, then mumbled, "Yes, but—"

I thought of the plantation being bought up for pennies on the dollar by Yankee carpetbaggers. I thought of the old black slave that had nowhere to go. I thought of the livery stolen from the old man because he couldn't afford taxes bordering on highway robbery, taxes that were levied by Yankee carpetbaggers. I turned back to my steak and over my shoulder, replied, "Tell Mr. Rawlings that as soon as I have another drink and a cigar I'll be finished. Shouldn't take more'n fifteen minutes."

For several seconds, the stunned headwaiter stammered and stuttered then scurried away. I kept my eyes on my table, pausing to pour another tumbler of Old Crow. I wasn't sure what to expect but I figured Rawlings to be the sort of jasper who was used to getting his way.

I was right. Moments later, I noticed someone stop at my table. I looked up into the cold eyes of a rock-jawed hombre who looked as out of place in his evening clothes as a hurdy-gurdy gal in a Baptist Women's Bible Class. He growled, "Mr. Rawlings wants this table, cowboy."

With the physical skills I learned from the Kiowa combined with the physical prowess I gained in setting up and tearing down the circus, physical confrontations never intimidated me. I grinned amiably and glanced across the room at the scowling man. "Reckon Rawlings over there is not only a rude jasper but he's also hard of hearing. I sent word I'd be finished here when I'm finished, friend, so go back and tell your fat boss what I said."

He was fast. In the next instant, his fingers dug into my shoulder and yanked me to my feet. Before he could make another move, I slammed my boot heel into his kneecap, bending his leg the way it wasn't supposed to bend.

He screamed and grabbed his leg, and while he was bouncing around on one foot I grabbed his arm with one hand, the seat of his pants with another, spun him around, and sent him smashing headfirst through the window to sprawl on the sidewalk outside.

The dining room grew quiet as a horse thief after a hanging, all eyes fixed on me. Taking my time, I poured another drink, downed it, lit a cigar, took my time putting on my Stetson, flipped a gold eagle on the table, tossed my soogan over my shoulder, and sauntered from the dining room, not even bothering to glance at the fuming Mr. Rawlings as I passed.

Once I stepped outside the Chilton House, I looked up and down the sidewalk, then broke into a mad dash for the corner, hoping to put enough distance between me and the Chilton to steer clear of any further quarrels.

Around the first corner I slowed to a fast walk to avoid any attention, crossed the street, and took the next corner. The train station was only three blocks distant so I made a wide circle and came in from the south side of the station.

The station was a large brick building with parapets around the top, reminding me of pictures of those medieval castles in the books in the professor's wagon. If I wasn't handling the ribbons as we traveled from town to town, I was reading.

I paused outside the station door and peered through a window. Only a handful of travelers were inside, some slumped on the worn benches sleeping, others visiting among themselves, and still others just staring numbly into space.

The large clock on the wall read 9:15. Forty-five minutes before my train pulled out for Knoxville. I looked over my shoulder. A few baggage clerks were pushing dollies loaded with luggage onto the platform.

I peered back inside and froze. Two uniformed police had entered the station, making a concentrated effort to speak to every person in the station.

"Blast!" I muttered. I turned to leave and came face to face with two more unsmiling policemen.

One of them patted his nightstick into the palm of his hand threateningly. "We been looking for you, cowboy."

I played the innocent. "Me? For what? I was just waiting to catch the train to Philadelphia." That was a lie but I'd learned long ago to never let anyone see the hand you're playing.

The other one jabbed me in the side with his stick. "Don't hand us that. There ain't no one else in Richmond wearing a black ten-gallon hat, a leather vest, and sporting a scar on his right cheek." He glanced at my waist. "You ain't wearing no iron?"

With wide-eyed innocence, I shook my head. "Don't believe in firearms, officer."

They grinned at each other. "You're coming with us, cowboy."

From the look in their eyes and the tone in their voices, I knew I couldn't talk my way out of this pickle. I shrugged. "Whatever you say, officer. I sure don't want to cause no trouble."

My pacifying tone relaxed them. One of them grunted, "Wait here with him, Homer. I'll get the wagon."

A few minutes later, a paddy wagon rattled around the corner of the station and reined up in front of us. Homer gestured to the barred door. "In there."

From the seat, his partner called out, "Need any help?"

"Nope. This old boy's real cooperating."

I opened the door and climbed inside.

Homer climbed in and closed the door behind us. He sat on one side of the wagon and gestured for me to sit on the other side.

The wagon lurched forward, rattling over the cobblestone streets. I didn't know how much time I had but I knew if they got me to the station I'd never catch that ten o'clock train. I cleared my throat. "You think this will take long? I'm supposed to catch the morning train out to Philadelphia."

He shrugged. "Depends."

I leaned back. My heart thudded against my chest. I dragged the tip of my tongue over my lips.

Rounding a corner, the wagon lurched, tossing us around.

The driver called out. "You okay in there?"

Homer looked up. "Yeah. Fine."

Before he looked back, I caught his uplifted jaw with a right uppercut, then quickly opened the door and jumped out, hoping I hadn't busted anything on him.

Chapter Three

 B y the time I reached the station the ten o'clock train was loading. I found a dark nook beneath the platform at the far end of the station and waited.

Moments later, half a dozen police swarmed over the station, searching the cavernous building and the train. I crouched lower in the shadows.

Two of them paused on the platform just above my head. "I didn't figure he would be here," muttered one whose voice I recognized as the driver of the paddy wagon.

Homer grunted, and slurring his words, he muttered, "He's heading for Philadelphia. Don't worry, I'll be here in the morning when he shows up. Ain't no man going to bust my jaw and get away with it."

The first voice replied, "You sure you feel all right, Homer? Your jaw is sure swelled up something fierce."

Homer snorted.

I peered over the edge of the platform as they walked away. Five minutes later, the engineer blew the whistle, the conductor looked up and down the platform, waved to the engineer, and then stepped onto the caboose.

Black smoke smelling like fried onions poured from the stack and the large four-foot wheels spun for traction. The gaudy four-four-zero engine lurched forward, gaining speed with each passing moment. I waited until the first passenger car was only a few feet away then stepped from the shadows and onto the steps.

After switching from rails to stage three times during the night, I finally climbed aboard the *General Grant* at sunrise for the reminder of the journey. I settled back on my bench and slept all the way into Knoxville where the ET&V—East Tennessee and Virginia Railway—had an hour layover before resuming its journey down to Chattanooga.

The café in the train station was doing a booming business. I slid on to a stool at the counter and ordered coffee. I grimaced when I sipped it. It tasted like watered down mud and was about the same consistency. But it was hot. I sipped it and stared anxiously out the window at the shiny rails that led to Chattanooga.

Chattanooga! That was where us boys in butternut

were laying siege to the city in 1863 when my life fell apart.

Brown's Ferry on the Tennessee River was where it happened. I was a captain serving under Colonel John Benjamin Avery who ordered me to hold my company in reserve for the night attack on Brown's Ferry. The only witness to the verbal order was Corporal Hugh Garrett, a messenger for Avery. While I respectfully questioned the colonel's decision stating that we needed every man we could muster, I did as he ordered.

After the defeat, General Bragg was screeching like a plucked bluejay and looking for blood. He found me. Colonel Avery was dead, and Corporal Garrett, whom I had never laid eyes on until the night Colonel Avery gave me my orders, had a sudden attack of deafness. He heard no such order.

The only reason I didn't get a firing squad for dereliction of duty in time of war was that several of Bragg's staff were my character witnesses. I figure Bragg and his cohorts thought I might be telling the truth but since Garrett testified against me, and since the Army needed an example for the rest of the Confederate troops who were in general growing antsy over the outcome of the war, they made me forfeit my pay, handed me a dishonorable discharge, and left me with the clothes on my back.

A middle-aged man striding through the café and announcing the departure of the Chattanooga train in five minutes interrupted my thoughts.

*   *   *

During the layover, the *General Grant* had added two passenger cars, the interiors so arranged that the double seats faced one another.

The smoky cars were crowded but I found a double seat occupied by a young boy across from his sister and his mother, next to an older gent I figured to be the boy's grandpa.

I nodded to the empty seat. "You mind company?"

The middle-aged man grinned easily. His voice boomed jovially. "Help yourself, stranger, help yourself.'

"Obliged." I slid my soogan under the bench and sat, smiling uncomfortably at my new traveling companions.

"Name's Floyd Coulter," he said, extending a work-scarred hand the size of a Virginia ham. "This here's my wife, Lucinda, and her youngsters Callie and Ben."

I took his hand. He had a powerful grip, the kind that comes from hard work, a grip that belied the black suit he wore. "Howdy there, Mr. Coulter. JC Thornton." I nodded to his wife, who was fair-complexioned with bright red hair. "Miz Coulter."

She smiled briefly, her pale green eyes coolly acknowledging me.

The boy, Ben, who I figured was about six or seven, stared at me, his wide eyes sliding up from the scar on my cheek to my wide-brimmed hat. "Are you from Texas, Mr. Thornton?"

Mrs. Coulter shushed him. "Hush now, Ben. It isn't polite to ask questions that are none of your business. Just you sit back and leave Mr. Thornton alone, you hear?" Her gentle southern drawl was sweet as honey and soft as goose down.

Subdued, the boy nodded and muttered. "Yes, ma'am."

Coulter laughed. "Let the boy be, Lucy. He's just curious."

I winked at Coulter and grinned at the boy. "Yep. I'm from Texas, and that's where I'm heading now, boy."

Ben's eyes lit up. His voice bubbled with enthusiasm. "That's where we're going. Texas. Floyd has a ranch in—" He hesitated and turned a hopeful eye on Coulter.

I couldn't help noticing the boy called the man Floyd, not Pa, and when Coulter introduced his wife, he said 'her' youngsters not 'their' youngsters.

"Kimble County," Coulter answered. "We filed on two miles of frontage on the Llano River somewhere near Silver Creek according to my brother. We're going in partners on it. You know where it is?"

I shot a furtive glance at Lucy Coulter, but she was staring out the window, from time to time waving her hand in front of her face to fan away some of the cigar smoke filling the car. I tried to keep my concern over his announcement from showing in my voice. "Yep. Right pretty country out there."

Coulter gushed. "That's what Sam said. Sam, he's my brother. He lives at Alta Springs in Falls County some piece back east of the Llano River."

At that moment, Callie tugged on her mother's arm. "Mama, Mama. I'm hungry."

Ben chimed in. "Me too."

Coulter laughed. "Might as well fetch me a sandwich too, Lucy. How about you, Thornton?"

"No, thanks." I pushed to my feet. "Reckon I'll amble outside for a cigarette."

Lucy Coulter glanced up at me, a brief flicker of appreciation in her eyes.

"I'll join you, Thornton. I could use a breath of fresh air."

Lucy Coulter whispered to him and nodded to his coat pocket. He guffawed. "Don't worry none. I won't."

Outside on the observation platform between the two cars, I pulled out a bag of Bull Durham and built a cigarette while Coulter pulled a pint bottle of whiskey from his coat pocket and popped the cork. He took a long swig and dragged the back of his hand across his lips. "Lucy gets upset if she sees me take a drink. I tell her that sometimes a man's got to have a drink. It's his right." He offered me the bottle.

I touched a match to my cigarette. "No thanks. Maybe later. It's too early for me to get started."

We both laughed.

I grew serious. "It isn't any of my business, Coulter, but what do you know about Kimble County?"

He looked at me curiously. "Good water, good grass, land there for the taking. That's what Sam says. What else is there to know?"

Dryly I replied, "It might help to know that the

Comanche and Kiowa are running wild out there. That's their stomping grounds, from San Antone to Santa Fe."

He eyed me narrowly, almost like I had offended him by telling him the truth. "If they was that bad, why didn't Sam say something about them?"

All I could do was shrug. "Look, Coulter. You're a likable gent, and you got yourself a fine little family. I just figured you should know what you're going to run into out there. I'm certainly not trying to offend you."

The craggy-faced man studied me another moment, then grinned. "I appreciate the advice, Thornton. I'll keep it in mind, but"—he patted his midriff—"I've sold out everything. It's all right here, under my shirt, so you see, we got no choice."

I shrugged. I'd done all I could.

The day dragged, what with the numerous stops for water and wood for the engine. I looked ahead to Chattanooga anxiously, wondering how I would feel being so close to the area that had changed my life forever.

Throughout the day, Lucy Coulter wore a calm and composed expression on her face. It was the kind of unreadable expression I could never hold in a poker game, especially if I was staring at the winning cards in my hand.

But, as we approached Chattanooga, her composure seemed to crumble. From time to time, she dabbed at her eyes with a lacy handkerchief. Even Ben grew solemn.

As we clattered across the Moccasin Bend of the Tennessee River into Chattanooga, I peered out the window, vainly trying to somehow peer through the mountains at Brown's Ferry.

When we laid over in Chattanooga, Coulter accompanied me outside to pick up some hot food for Lucy and the children. He shook his head while we waited at the counter for our orders. "Be glad when we leave this place behind."

I arched an eyebrow. "Why's that?"

He nodded to the train. "Lucy's husband, the kids' pa. He was killed at Brown's Ferry five years ago when the Three-Seventy-Seventh Louisiana Rebs attacked."

All I could do was gape at him.

Chapter Four

The warning whistle of the train cut through the confusion in my head.

"Here you are, gents," said a smiling waitress when she slid two brown paper sacks across the counter to us. "Meat and cheese sandwiches and pickled eggs. Sorry we ain't got nothing hot."

Jovially, Coulter thanked the waitress and headed back to the train. "Let's go, Thornton, or we'll get left behind."

The train had started moving when we reached the loading dock. "Run for it!" Coulter shouted.

We raced across the dock and leaped aboard, pausing to catch our breath. Coulter started inside but I laid my hand on his arm. "I reckon I need to find me another spot to sit."

He looked at me in surprise then puzzlement. "I don't understand. What's going on?"

"You know how times are now. The war was over three years ago, but folks always come back to it sooner or later, wanting to know which side a jasper was on. Me, I was on the losing side."

Coulter nodded. "Being from Texas, I figured you was. I was too."

I blinked, confused. "You, a Reb? But Mrs. Coulter. You said her husband was killed at Brown's Ferry by the Rebs."

"Lucy and her husband was from West Virginia what turned Federal and split away from Virginia. We lived about half a mile apart. Knowed each other for years. After the war . . . well, life goes on. Lucy had two children. My wife had died of consumption, so we just decided to team up." He paused, arched an eyebrow, and laughed. "So you see, Thornton, you ain't no worser a heathen than me."

Shaking my head, I replied wryly. "I don't know about that, Coulter. I was a captain in the Three-Seventy-Seventh Louisiana."

His jaw dropped open.

I nodded.

He grew serious. "I suppose I see what you mean, Thornton. Maybe you're right. I don't know about things like that anymore. It never made sense to me."

"One thing I'd like for you to know, Coulter. My company was held out of the battle. While the fighting was taking place, I was a mile back on Wilson's Bluff overlooking Brown's Ferry."

He studied me a moment, then held out his hand. "Thanks for telling me but I wish you hadn't. I never kept secrets from my wife, not Dora, or Lucy." He paused. "Maybe she'll just let it lie."

I grinned sheepishly. "Well, at least if she finds out, we won't have to be staring at each other across four feet of open space."

I made an excuse to Lucy Coulter that I had run across some trail hands from Texas in the forward car.

In the next car, all the seats faced the same way. It was an older car so the suspension wasn't as stable as the newer ones, which meant a more noticeable swaying as the car passed over uneven rails.

I found a spot next to a dapper gent who was leaning up against the window sound asleep. I stowed my soogan under the bench and sat, stretching my long legs under the seat ahead of me and folding my arms across my chest.

During the night, I rose and headed for the rear door for a breath of fresh air and a cigarette. Through the door window on the next car, I saw Coulter talking to a rough-looking gent who had taken my seat.

I remembered the bottle of whiskey Coulter carried. I grinned. I wouldn't mind a stiff jolt about now.

*   *   *

Next morning at our layover in Birmingham, I got off to stretch my legs. While I was enjoying a cigarette, I spotted Lucy Coulter heading in my direction with her two children in tow. When she spotted me her green eyes blazed. She tilted her slender jaw and stalked past, leaving behind a wake of ice that froze me to the bone.

I shook my head wryly. She knew.

Right then, I knew I wasn't looking forward to the remainder of the trip to Fort Worth. In fact, I considered laying over for a few days in Meridian, Mississippi before continuing on to Jackson and Vicksburg.

While I stood there studying her retreating back, a woman's voice cut through the screech of iron wheels against steel rails and the melee of chatter among the arriving and departing passengers.

"JC! JC Thornton!"

Frowning, I looked around. Across the loading dock, a buxom woman in a high-necked princess dress, cinched in at the waist and the hem dragging on the platform, waved at me. She wore a huge floppy brimmed hat with what looked like a bushel of flowers on top.

I blinked once or twice, then recognized Mary Hannah Jordan, who had owned a fancy parlor house in Missoula, Montana. I'd met her two years before when I helped drift a few hundred head of beef on up to Montana for some rich Englishman who was trying to start a ranch.

I grinned. "Hannah!"

She raced across the dock and threw herself in my

arms. I spun her around like a feather. Although she was ten years my senior, she had not lost her teenage body nor her laughing eyes.

"What in the blazes are you doing here?" she exclaimed when I set her down.

"Heading back to Texas. What about you?"

"Going down to Meridian." Her eyes twinkled mischievously. "Investing in a boardinghouse down there."

I chuckled. "Knowing you, it'll be a fancy one."

She laughed throatily. "Fancier than any Mississippi has ever seen."

"Well, come on," I said, taking her arm. "Let's find us a seat. We got a lot of catching up to do."

The laughter faded from her face. "Sorry, honey." She glanced around. "I'm riding with a . . . a friend. He's investing in my boardinghouse. You understand?" She arched an impish eyebrow.

I cradled her chin in the crook of my finger and tilted it up. "You bet I do." I winked at her and released her dainty chin. "Good luck."

She blew me a kiss. "Come see me next time through Meridian, you hear? We'll talk over old times and maybe make some new ones."

At that moment, an older gent toting around an enormous belly beneath a four-button chesterfield coat approached. He cleared his throat. Hannah smiled, curled her arm through his like silk, and glibly lied. "George, meet my cousin, JC Thornton. JC, this is George L Meeks, the most handsome man in Birmingham."

As the mismatched couple headed for the train, Floyd Coulter stopped at my side, a sheepish look on his face. "Lucy wormed it out of me, Thornton. Blasted sorry about that."

Hannah glanced over her shoulder and waved. I waved back and my eyes still fixed on Hannah, spoke to Coulter. "Nothing to be sorry about. I reckon everyone handles his own feelings the way he sees fit." I turned to him. "I'll stay up in my car. No sense in stirring up sorrowful memories every time she sees me."

A few hours out of Birmingham, the passenger car lurched to the right as we passed over an uneven rail. A passenger in the aisle bumped against my shoulder but continued on his way. He was the same rough-looking jasper who had taken my seat with the Coulters.

Several seats ahead, he stopped and spoke to two other hombres, one with a full beard, and the other so ugly he must have been in the outhouse when lightning struck.

I thought nothing of it at the time.

An hour later the train ground to a halt to load firewood onto the tender. A gust of air swept through the car. I looked up and saw Hannah standing in the open doorway surveying the passengers. When she spotted me she nodded briefly, stepped back onto the platform and let the door swing shut.

Fishing my bag of Bull Durham from a vest pocket, I ambled to the door. She was standing outside, waiting for me. Before I could say a word, she said, "That man you was talking to on the loading dock back in Birmingham—he a friend of yours?"

Her question caught me by surprise. I had to think a moment. "You mean Coulter? Just met him. Why? You know him?"

She glanced over her shoulder nervously. "No, but I know a couple other jaspers on this train. They're low-down polecats that wouldn't hesitate to steal the last piece of bread out of a starving baby's mouth. And one of them has been getting mighty well acquainted with that friend of yours."

I frowned. "How do you know all this?"

Her dark eyes glinted like steel. "I know them from Knoxville and Chattanooga. I might be wrong, but you best caution Coulter to watch hisself around them."

At that moment the train lurched forward. Hannah tumbled into me. "Steady." I laughed. "You know proper women don't go around throwing themselves at strange men."

She looked up at me wickedly. "I'm not a proper woman."

Chapter Five

After Hannah left, I strolled to the far end of the passenger car and stepped out onto the platform. I pulled out my bag of Bull Durham and casually peered into the next car. My brows knit. The same hombre who had bumped into my shoulder earlier was palavering with Coulter just like they were long lost cousins.

Remembering just how friendly and talkative Coulter was, I figured by now those three hombres knew about the money belt the middle-aged man wore around his waist. And if Hannah was right, the thieves were planning on separating Coulter from his belt.

I built a cigarette, cupping the match flame against the wind whipping around the corner of the car.

Studying the burly jasper talking to Coulter, I tried to figure out if he was going to wait until the next stop, or if he would get him out on the platform under some pretense, take his belt, and kick him off the moving train.

Taking a last drag on my cigarette, I flipped it down between the two cars and went back inside where I could keep an eye on the two scruffy cowpokes in front of me. When they moved out I'd follow.

As the sun fell below the hills, the conductor made his way through the cars lighting the coal oil lanterns spaced every few feet on the wall above our heads.

The ceiling of the car above the lanterns was black from the soot given off by the burning wick. Despite half a dozen lanterns, shadows filled the car.

Sometime later, the moon rose, casting a pale white glow on the passing countryside. I was half asleep when I heard boots thumping on the floor. Through narrowed eyes, I saw the two cowpokes climbing from their seat and heading in my direction. Instantly I was alert. Then it dawned on me. The Tombigbee River was just ahead. What better way to get rid of a body than toss it in a river? I remained motionless as they passed.

When I heard the door open and close, I stretched my arms and struggled to my feet, feigning drowsiness. I fumbled for my Bull Durham as I lurched unsteadily down the rocking car toward the rear door.

A rough hand grabbed my shoulder. "Where do you think you're going, cowboy?" The jasper with the full beard glared at me.

At that moment, the train hit the bridge across the

Tombigbee River. With a casual grin, I nodded to the door. "Figured on a breath of fresh air and a cigarette." Behind him, I spotted a flash of light as the door on the other car opened.

He grunted. "Go out the other way. This door's jammed."

"No problem," I muttered, turning back. At the same time, I shucked my sixgun and spun back around, slamming the barrel across the side of his head.

He dropped like a sack of Arbuckle's Coffee.

I stepped outside just in time to see the ugly jasper rip the money belt from Coulter's waist. The end of the belt whipped back toward me. I grabbed it and gave it a jerk, yanking the surprised cowpoke around.

Before he could utter a sound, I busted him across the face with the muzzle of my Colt. He screeched and doubled over, grabbing at his nose. I gave him a kick in the rear, sending him head over heels off the bridge and into the river, the same fate he'd planned for Coulter.

I turned my Colt on the third gent, who threw up his hands and screeched, "Don't shoot, don't shoot."

Deliberately, I cocked the hammer. "You got a choice. Jump or digest a lead plum."

He jumped.

Coulter stood staring at me in disbelief as the train rocked along on the rails. I held out the money belt. "Reckon this is yours."

He stepped across to my platform. "Where in the

Sam Hill did you come from?" he asked as he slipped the belt under his shirt and fastened it. "I thought I was deader than a beaver hat."

I holstered my sixgun. "Just a minute." Opening the door, I dragged the unconscious cowpoke onto the platform.

Coulter frowned in concern. "You're not going to throw him off, are you?"

I looked at Coulter in surprise. "That's what he planned for you."

"I know but he's unconscious."

I chuckled. "Then he won't feel it when he lands."

The older man shook his head. "I know what you say is right, but at least let him wake up."

Pursing my lips, I studied Floyd Coulter. I couldn't help thinking his suggestion was like nursing a sick rustler back to health before you hang him. "You're too decent a jasper for your own good, Coulter. Out here, you can't trust folks like neighbors back in Virginia. Out here, one half of the population is trying to figure out how to swindle the other half of their belongings."

Coulter grimaced. "I might be a heap of things, Thornton, but I'm not dumb enough not to pay attention to advice from those with more experience than I got, and I'm not so ungrateful as not to want to shake your hand."

We shook, and at that moment, the train started slowing for another load of firewood.

The bearded cowpoke was still unconscious when we stopped, but I kicked him off anyway after shucking his sixgun and sticking it under my belt. Coulter didn't argue.

We were almost in Jackson, Mississippi when I awakened. I was stiff and hungry and looking forward to a few minutes in the war-torn city.

In the station, I spotted the Coulters. Floyd nodded, Ben waved, Callie clung to her mama's dress, and Lucy ignored me.

I was starting to grow antsy as we rolled through Vicksburg and across the Mississippi River. Another few hundred miles and we would be in Fort Worth. I couldn't help wondering just where Hugh Garrett was at that moment.

Trying to locate him in Arizona Territory would be like finding a fleck of gold mixed with a wheelbarrow full of sand. But, I reminded myself, it would be done, one grain at a time. All it demanded was patience and determination, two qualities I was learning the hard way.

Finally, we rolled into Shreveport, Louisiana, and right into the proverbial hornet's nest.

Rail service to Fort Worth had been interrupted. A flood the previous week had washed out the bridge over the Red River along with several miles of rails. The only means of transportation was ferrying the river, then stagecoach to Marshall where we would once again board the train to Fort Worth.

I've never understood the fickleness of fate. My

Kiowa father laughed that fate was always playing jokes on us, and the sooner we laughed at the jokes, the sooner we would forget our problems.

It took some doing to remember his advice when I climbed into the stagecoach and came face-to-face with Floyd Coulter and his family.

I paused halfway into the stage, my ears burning, my cheeks flushed. "I–I'm sorry. I'll take the next stage."

Coulter stopped me. "Nonsense. Ride with us. The next stage won't be until tomorrow."

I glanced sheepishly at Lucy Coulter.

Her gaze was chilly. "My husband is right, Mr. Thornton. He told me how you prevented those men from taking our savings. I—we would be pleased for your company."

Callie scrambled from the seat and slipped in by her mother. Ben looked up at me with a wide grin. "Will you tell me about Texas, Mr. Thornton, huh? Will you?"

After an hour or so, despite the bouncing and swaying of the stagecoach on its leather thoroughbraces, Ben dozed off. Callie lay sleeping with her head in her mama's lap. Lucy stared out the window.

"Beautiful country out here," Coulter said. "I didn't figure Texas had so many trees. I always heard it was wide open."

I grinned. "That's coming. Believe me. Why, there's land out there so flat and wide open that you can see a campfire from ten miles at night."

He guffawed. "You're pulling my leg."

"No, sir. I haven't been all over it, but from what I've seen, I figure the good Lord might have been planning on settling down in Texas Himself."

From the corner of my eye, I spotted Lucy glance at me for a moment. I continued. "There's trees for cabins, water for drinking, wild game for eating, and grass higher than your head for cows. Why, I've even heard it said that some of the grass is so thick and rich that you can grow a two-year-old calf in six months."

Coulter roared and, for a fleeting moment, a tiny smile played over Lucy Coulter's lips. "What's it like where we're going? You've been there, haven't you?"

I studied him a moment. From the look in his eyes, I knew he remembered my warning about the Comanche and Kiowa. "Good country. Plenty of space, plenty of water."

Ben sat up. Our conversation must have awakened him, for he asked. "Will there be any Indians?"

When I didn't answer immediately, Lucy looked around at me, a puzzled frown knitting her forehead.

Coulter cleared his throat and shot her a furtive glance. "Some, but nothing to worry about. Sam would have told me."

Lucy's face grew hard. Her eyes turned an icy green, like winter ice on some of the Tennessee streams I'd seen a few years earlier. "Is that right, Mr. Thornton?"

I hated to cause trouble between a wife and husband, but I would have hated even more to see them lying on the ground scalped. I supposed if anyone was to blame for the situation it had to be Sam Coulter for painting a picture that was nothing like the real thing.

"Well, ma'am. I'm just a naturally suspicious jasper. Now, I haven't been out yonder since we pushed cattle up from South Texas last spring. About April, I reckon. This here's October. A heap can change in six months."

Her eyes narrowed with a suspicious glint. "You didn't answer my question, Mr. Thornton. Are there Indians, and is there danger?"

I glanced at Coulter whose eyes were pleading with me. "Truth is, Miz Coulter, the Kiowa are unsettled right now. Little Mountain, their chief since the eighteen-thirties died a couple years back. Satanta took over and led a few raids against the white man. Sitting Bear is a peaceful chief, so the two of them, Satanta and Sitting Bear, are usually at odds with each other."

She studied me a moment. "You talk like you know them, Mr. Thornton."

"Yes, ma'am. I lived with the Kiowa until I was about twelve."

Chapter Six

Whille my announcement silenced Floyd and Lucy Coulter, it opened up floodgates of excited questions from young Ben. I spent the next hour or so explaining that Indian children do not go to school within four walls but in the outdoors. "Their education is real life experience." I winked at Coulter. "Sometimes they learn the hard way, but they learn. And no," I added, "they can't spell like you can."

I went on to explain why warriors painted their faces and the meaning of the various colors. "Black means death; red is power and success as well as war; blue means defeat and trouble; and yellow is joy and bravery."

"What about white?"

"And white means peace."

41

We rolled into Marshall, Texas only minutes before the train was pulling out for Fort Worth. On the loading dock, I extended my hand to Coulter. "Good luck to you." I nodded to Lucy and winked at the children.

Coulter frowned. "Ain't you going on to Fort Worth?"

I glanced at his wife and gestured to the car behind the tender. "I'm riding up there."

Lucy just stared at me with that same unreadable expression. A wry grin of understanding on his face, Coulter grunted, "Good luck to you, and thanks again for all the help."

When I settled into my seat minutes later, I figured I would never see the Coulters again.

Then fate played another joke on me.

A couple hours later, about sundown, a hand touched my shoulder. I looked up and my jaw dropped open when I saw Lucy Coulter looking down at me. Her wooden face was lined with concern and worry.

I jumped to my feet. "Miz Coulter."

A self-conscious smile ticked up one side of her lips. "Mr. Thornton. I–I wonder if I might speak with you a moment."

I grimaced inwardly, figuring she was going to lay into me about her dead husband. "Yes, ma'am." I gestured to the empty bench beside me. "Please, have a seat."

With a short nod, she sat on the edge of the seat, scooted around so she could face me. I could see the uncertainty in her eyes. "I'm sorry about the war, Miz Coulter."

She squeezed her tiny hands together. Hesitantly, she replied. "I know I have not been a pleasant person the last several days, Mr. Thornton, but passing through the city where my children's father died and then learning you were in the Army that killed him, I–I"—she bit her bottom lip—"well, it was too much for me to handle."

I grinned. "I reckon I'd feel the same way, ma'am." I figured she was just trying to clear her conscience for what she considered a violation of the proper behavior of the southern women.

And then fate played another joke on me.

"But that isn't the reason I'm here, Mr. Thornton." She paused. "The real reason I'm here is that I would like for you to accompany us to my brother-in-law's home in Falls County."

I've seen hail the size of cantaloupes fall from the sky; I've seen cats chasing dogs; and I once saw a drover pull a two-headed snake out of his bedroll, but I've never had anything surprise me more than Lucy Coulter's request.

She continued before I could fashion a reply. "I know you're headed for Arizona, and I know I'm asking you to delay your journey, but, as surprising as it might seem, Mr. Thornton, I trust you. I, ah, I don't know if I like you, because of the war and all, but I do trust you. Mr. Coulter is a good man, a good husband, and the best father he knows how to be to my children. But coming to a wild and unsettled country is a new experience for him. He has never faced anything like we have ahead of us."

She hesitated, staring deep into my eyes, trying to read what was on my mind, which at that moment, because of the complete confusion in my head, was an impossible task for anyone.

One part of me was thrilled by her request, but another part was disinclined because of the delay in finding Hugh Garrett. "Well, Miz Coulter, I—"

She pushed to her feet abruptly. "Don't give me an answer now. You think on it. Let me know in Fort Worth. If I don't hear from you, I'll know you decided to continue your own journey."

I studied her a moment. "What does Mr. Coulter have to say?"

A light blush tinged his cheeks. She dropped her gaze to her hands in her lap, then lifted it to stare at me defiantly. "I haven't told him yet."

"He might not like the idea."

A knowing smile played over her lips. "Floyd would give his own life for us, Mr. Thornton. I love him for that. If he knows I'll feel more comfortable with you along he won't think twice about it."

I arched an eyebrow as she walked away. Lucy Coulter was not the passive little southern belle I first thought.

The remainder of the ride into Fort Worth took eight hours, the longest eight hours I've ever lived. I changed my mind a dozen times.

The closer we got to Fort Worth, the more I found my-self trying to figure the best route south to Falls County, which was just beyond Waco.

I came up with a dozen explanations as to why I should head on out to Arizona, but I couldn't turn my back on the Coulter family. And unless they found some dependable hands down in Alta Springs with Sam Coul-ter, I knew I would be accompanying them on to Kim-ble County. It just wasn't in me to let some innocents get themselves killed. Besides, Garrett would be there when I was ready.

The professor would understand and so would Big Horse, my Kiowa father.

Coulter was as tickled as a flea in a doghouse when I announced I would take them on down to Falls County if he wanted. "Reckon you'll need a good rig," I explained as we waited for their luggage to be unloaded. "Mules is your best bet. Put your family in a boardinghouse, and we'll amble over to the livery and see what we can find."

The jaspers at the first two liveries were so crooked you couldn't tell by their tracks if they were coming or going. When we walked into the third livery I jerked to a halt, peering at the bowlegged cowpoke bent over in-specting a horseshoe with his backend to us.

"Wishbone. Is that you?"

The young cowpoke looked under his arm at us. When he recognized me, he dropped the hoof and stomped through the horse biscuits and cow patties toward us, a grin as wide as the Brazos and his hand stuck out. "Well, I'll be hornswoggled. JC Thornton. I never expected to see you so soon. It's only been a few weeks since you pulled out of Dodge." He paused, then asked, "Any luck?"

I shook my head, we palavered a few moments, then I introduced him to Coulter and told him what we wanted.

He grinned. "I only been here a week or so, but I know just what you're looking for." He pointed to a corral beyond the barn. "Come on with me. You too, Mr. Coulter."

I nodded to Coulter. "I'm warning you, Wishbone, we're not packing enough money to burn a wet mule."

Wishbone laughed. "Old Chester, he's the owner. He's a honest old jasper who'll charge you fair price. And the stock I'm agoing to show you, why, there ain't none any better this side of Montana." He glanced over his shoulder at Coulter. "What kind of plunder are you carrying?"

Coulter frowned at me. I explained. "Household goods. Furniture. That sort of thing."

The older man shook his head. "We're traveling light. Figure we'd buy what we needed when we go there."

Wishbone grinned. "Reckon you won't need no Conestoga. A prairie schooner would suit your needs. Ten, twelve feet long, four wide. Six mules."

Wishbone was as good as his promise. The prairie schooner was in good shape and sported a double Osnaburg canvas top stretched over four bowed hickory supports. Three spans of mules with two strong wheelers and a couple smart leaders were, as Wishbone bragged, the best this side of Montana.

We spent the next day picking up supplies and packing the wagon. Wishbone put me on to a four-year-old dun gelding with a deep chest and long legs. For another double gold eagle, he threw in a worn but well-built center fire saddle.

That night, Wishbone and me put ourselves around thick steaks at a sort of going away supper, then ambled across the street to the White Elephant Saloon for drink and a hand of poker.

The White Elephant was one of those saloons where a jasper minded his own business and if he accidentally made eye contact with anyone, he smiled and looked away.

Up and down the cattle trails, cowpokes, worn to a nub from a day in the saddle and covered with caked dust, lay on their soogans at night and related the far-fetched stories they'd heard about the White Elephant.

The whiskey was good but it wasn't cheap. I sipped my drink.

Wishbone shook his head. "Sorry you didn't find Garrett."

I rubbed the scar on my cheek. "He's supposed to be in Arizona. That's where I'm heading, once I take care of my business with the Coulters." I leaned back and grinned at Wishbone. "You wintering here?"

The amiable young cowpoke shrugged. "Reckoned on it. My folks want me to, but I don't cotton to the cold up here." He grinned sheepishly. "I like them warm days along the Rio Grande down in South Texas."

I laughed. "Come on with us. We're heading on down past Waco to a little place called Alta Springs where Coulter's brother lives. From there, it's just a short piece on down to Harrisburg and South Texas for you."

He studied me a moment. "What about Mr. Coulter? Reckon he would mind?"

Leaning forward, I replied, "To tell you the truth, he'd welcome an army." I paused and added. "Where he's going, he'll probably need one."

Frowning, Wishbone muttered, "I didn't know there was much trouble down around Waco. At least, I ain't heard of it."

I took another sip of whiskey. "He isn't stopping at Alta Springs. He's heading on out to Kimble County."

Wishbone's eyes grew wide, and he leaned back and whistled softly. "He's asking for a heap of trouble." The younger cowpoke shook his head. "I ain't going out there, but I'd still appreciate riding down to Alta Springs with you all."

"Come ahead. We're pulling out with the sun."

Chapter Seven

Typical of Texas weather, Mother Nature forgot it was October and that it was supposed to be cool, not sweltering, which it was every single day for the next week or so until we reached the Brazos River just north of Waco.

We found a small grove of trees that offered a shady respite from the blistering sun and some graze for the mules. "From here on," I said, "we'll follow the Brazos on down to Alta Springs."

Ben paused with an armload of dry branches he had gathered for the fire and frowned up at me. "What kind of name is that, Brazos?"

"Indian name, boy. Means crooked." His frown deepened. "This here river is said to be the crookedest one in Texas. I don't know about that but that's what's said, and that's why the Indians give her that name."

Lucy Coulter looked up from the iron spider in which she was mixing up the evening meal, a trace of a smile on her lips as she looked at her son. "You best hurry up now, Ben, if you want supper tonight." She glanced at me. While she didn't smile, at least I didn't see the cool look in her eyes that was usually reserved for me.

Wishbone fit right in with the Coulters and their youngsters, and by the time we reached Waco, I figured he was probably there for the journey all the way out to Kimble County, despite his misgivings.

That night around the fire, sipping after-supper coffee and enjoying a cigarette, I grinned at Wishbone when the young cowpoke started complaining about the unseasonable heat of the last couple weeks.

"Better be careful, Wishbone. Old Mother Nature might get tired of your complaining and throw us a Blue Norther."

Ben, who had been sitting back and listening to the grownups talk about the journey and what was to come, spoke up. "What's a Blue Norther?"

I chuckled. "Sometimes out here, a mighty cold storm blows in from the north, so cold that it can turn a body the color of blue. That's why they call them Blue Northers." I glanced at his mother who smiled back briefly at the stretcher I was handing her son.

She shook her head at Ben, silently admonishing him to stop interrupting the grownups.

Coulter cleared his throat. "It's sure been mighty dry. A spell of rain wouldn't bother me."

Wishbone warned him. "Don't ask for no rain, Mr. Coulter. We got it good right now, what with the road hard–packed." He dug his spur into the hard ground, chipping out a few shards of the hardpan. "This dirt here gets wet, it turns to a sticky mud that'll clog the spokes of the wagon wheels. We'll be stopping every mile or so to clean off the mud."

Coulter frowned at me. I agreed. "He's right. The rest of our trip is along the river. All the water we want." I glanced at the thumbnail of a moon in the sky. "And I don't reckon we need to waste no time. I figure we'll get us some rain within three days. If we make good time, we ought to be only a couple days out of Alta Springs when it hits."

Wishbone grunted. "Two days of rain, huh? That won't be too bad."

Like all curious youngster, Ben couldn't hold his tongue. "I didn't know anybody could tell when it was going to rain. Is that some kind of Indian trick?"

I chuckled. "No, boy. Look. Up at the moon. See that white circle around it?"

"Yes, sir."

"Well, now, how many stars do you see in that circle?"

"Let me see . . . one, two, three. Three of them." He looked back at me, a frown on his face.

"The old timers say when there's a circle around the moon, the number of stars in the circle tells how long before the rain hits."

Little Ben studied me for a moment, wondering if I

was pulling his leg. He glanced at his ma and then at Coulter before eyeing me suspiciously.

I nodded. "It doesn't hold true all the time, but more often than not, you can count on those signs."

This time they held true, for three days later a driving rain struck in mid-afternoon with a vengeance. We buttoned down the canvas cover by closing the pucker holes. The double Osnaburg sheeting kept the interior fairly dry for Lucy Coulter and the children. Coulter, perched on the seat driving the team, was soaked just like Wishbone and me astride our ponies.

We made an early camp and strung up canvas flies to ward off the rain, which was turning cold. Wishbone glanced at me over the fire. I nodded. The next morning would have a little more than just a chill in it. I figured it would be right frosty.

Coulter sat close to the fire, warming himself against the shivers taking over his body. He began to cough—a deep, hacking cough.

During the night the rain stopped but the temperature dropped. Next morning, we rose early, our breath puffs in the crisp air. We built a large fire to ward off the chill. I went to hitch up the team. Coulter came to help but he was still coughing so I sent him back to the fire. "You'll be cold enough later on today. Best you stay warm while you can. Maybe you can give Wishbone a hand whipping up breakfast."

When Lucy and the children climbed out of the wagon, she looked at Wishbone in surprise. Wishbone grinned up at her. "Figured on giving you a break this morning, Miz Coulter." He nodded to the grub. "Fried bacon and johnnycakes." He wrapped a thin johnnycake around a couple slices of bacon, dipped it in the bacon grease remaining in the spider and smacked his lips. "Try it, ma'am. This grub will keep a body agoing all day."

Reluctantly, they tried the new fare, and after the first bite they dug into it.

The day was cold and overcast, the leaden sky threatening more rain. Just as Wishbone had predicted, we were forced to stop every mile or so to dig the mud from between the hickory spokes of the wheels so as not to tire the team unnecessarily.

Fortunately, the rain held off.

While the weather did not moderate, it grew no worse, but Coulter's cough grew no better. His skin took on a pallor, his heavy beard standing out in stark contrast to the pastiness of his face. From time to time, spasms of shivers shook his thick frame.

But, to his credit, he never complained. Lucy kept dosing him with patent medicines that didn't seem to do him any good.

The ground grew firmer and we made fair progress. Finally, two and a half weeks after we left Fort Worth, we pulled up in front of a log building about three times the size of a regular cabin. Smoke poured from a chimney at either end of the structure.

Wishbone swung down off his sorrel and ducked inside, returning seconds later with a wide grin on his face. "This here place is Alta Springs."

My hopes soared. Now I could leave the Coulters with kin, and go about my own business in running down Hugh Garrett.

With directions from the sutler inside, ten minutes later we were heading east along a narrow trace winding through a forest of oak and cedar. The north wind whipped through the trees, chilling me. I tugged my Mackinaw about me tighter.

With a hacking cough, Coulter called from the seat of the wagon. "There's a fork up ahead. Must be the one to Sam that jasper mentioned."

An hour later, we pulled out of the forest into a clearing of over fifty acres. Directly in front of us sat a neatly constructed log cabin with a dogtrot. Off to one side was a pole barn surrounded by a pole corral holding a few head of horses and a couple dozen head of cows.

The cabin door swung inward, and a one-legged man leaning on a homemade crutch hobbled out on the wooden plank porch and peered up at us. His eyes lit when he recognized Coulter. "Floyd? Is that you? Really you?"

Coulter bounded off the wagon and grabbed his brother's hand.

That night, another storm struck.

We sat in front of the stone fireplace, nice and snug, listening to the rain pound against the woodshake roof while the brothers caught up on family news, the two wives gossiped, and Ben and Callie played with their newfound cousins.

"I sent you a letter, Floyd," Sam explained, indicating his missing leg. "Telling you I couldn't make it out to Kimble County this year. Maybe next year when I heal up good."

Coulter glanced at Lucy and stifled a cough. "We didn't get it but no matter. I can go on out there and get things started, then you can come on out next spring."

Lucy Coulter glanced at me, her eyes filled with apprehension.

I grunted. "Best you tend that cough, Coulter. Winter weather out here can be something mighty fierce."

He shook his head. "I'm fine. I can do it." A spasm of coughing racked his body, doubling him over.

Sam Coulter glanced at me, then laughed. "Sure you can, little brother. Sure you can."

That night, Coulter and his family slept in the loft; Sam and his family in the bedroom across the dogtrot; and Wishbone and me on the floor in front of the fireplace.

During the night, Lucy arose several times to tend her husband who kept us awake with his coughing.

Next morning, she was pale and haggard from no sleep and a heap of worry. Her blue gingham dress was wrinkled. "I think he might have pneumonia," she mumbled when we inquired as to his health.

"One thing is certain," proclaimed Sam Coulter. "Floyd ain't heading out to Kimble County now." He nodded to Lucy. "You all might as well figure on staying here until spring. Ain't that right, Martha?" he added, turning to his wife.

Martha Coulter nodded emphatically. "Lordy, yes. There ain't no sense in you folks heading on."

Sam looked around at Wishbone and me. "You boys is welcome to stay on too if you're looking to winter somewhere. I got plenty of work here now that I'm hopping around on one leg. I ain't got no money, but I got plenty of grub and a warm house."

Wishbone looked at me hopefully.

I shook my head. "I'm obliged, Sam, but I reckon on heading out to Arizona Territory. I got business out there." I glanced at Lucy who was studying me curiously.

Wishbone grunted, "Reckon I'll take you up on that offer, Mr. Coulter. I figured on finding somewhere to hole up and then next spring, punch cattle up to Kansas or Colorado."

Chapter Eight

I was tightening the cinch on my center-fire rig when Wishbone came into the barn and leaned up against one of the stalls. He fished a bag of Bull Durham from his shirt pocket and starting building a cigarette. "Well, partner, you take care, you hear?"

"You're welcome to ride along if you want." I grinned.

He shook his head. "Too much of a ride for me." He glanced around. "I'll settle for here, but I'll keep my fingers crossed for you."

At that moment, Lucy Coulter emerged from the cabin with a oilskin-covered bundle in her hands and a heavy shawl around her shoulders against the cold. I swung into the saddle. Wishbone slapped me on the leg. "See you later, amigo." He headed back to the cabin, holding the corral gate open for Lucy, who stopped beside my dun.

"Biscuits and venison," she said simply, a worried look on her slender face. She paused, and the pale green of her eyes turned the color of moss green as the worried expression on her face grew deeper. "My husband told me on the train about what happened at Brown's Ferry. And this morning, Wishbone told me the same thing. I know where you're going, Mr. Thornton. I hope you'll be careful." She handed me the bundle. I reached for it, and for a moment, she refused to turn it loose. Then, with a sad smile, she released it and stepped back.

I rode away from the small farm with mixed feelings, feelings to which I had no right for she was a married woman. Still, she remained on my mind.

A week later, I rode into Kimble County and deliberately followed the Llano River. I didn't know where Coulter's land was situated but instantly saw that anywhere along the banks of the pristine river would be just about as close to a little bit of heaven as any hombre could hope for on this earth.

Around a graceful bend in the river, I reined up, spotting the stone ruins of a cabin on the crest of a nearby hill. With a click of my tongue, I urged my pony up the slight incline. I pulled up beside one of the fallen walls and surveyed the countryside.

I didn't know Sam Coulter all that well but I had to

hand it to him. He had stumbled across some might fetching country, this Llano River valley.

The water was pure and sweet, the grass, through winter dead, was lush and rich, and the rolling land seemed to stretch on forever between thick patches of live oak forest.

More than once in the next two months, I thanked Wishbone for the dun he sold me. Despite the cold weather, which kept most bands of Comanche and Kiowa holed up in their teepees and wickiups, on three different occasions I was forced to outdistance small war parties, the last only a few miles from Soldier's Farewell in Arizona Territory three or four days before reaching Tucson.

From El Paso west, through Fort Fillmore, Los Cruces, Dona Ana, and Cook's Springs, I inquired about Hugh Garrett, describing the hombre as I remembered him, about five-ten, a couple inches shorter than me, a lantern jaw, and two eyes set unnaturally close together. At Roblaro, between Dona Ana and Cook's Springs, the owner remembered the narrow-set eyes, but that had been three months earlier.

I rode out of Roblaro with my hopes high.

Absently, I rubbed the scar on my cheek. Patience and determination, I reminded myself, seeing the image of my Kiowa father, Big Horse, in my mind's eye. Patience and determination.

But try as I might, I couldn't help thinking about Lucy Coulter.

Four days later on the tail end of a cold front, I rode into Tucson, the capitol of the territory, and a city I'd often heard was Arizona's answer for Sodom and Gomorrah.

If the comparison was anywhere near accurate, then the two Biblical cities must have been cities of mudboxes, dingy and dilapidated, all cracked and baked with dust and filth, and the narrow streets littered with broken corrals, bake-ovens, shattered pottery, and carcasses of dead animals.

Apparently, the inhabitants had never heard of whitewash, for the winter sun baked down on unpainted adobes that appeared cheerless and desolate. From time to time as I wound through the narrow streets, black-eyed children, brown as the hard-packed soil, peered from the dark confines of the mud-houses.

Nearing the downtown section of the city, I noticed the adobe buildings began giving way to a few brick and clapboard buildings.

Like all western towns, for every general store there were two saloons; for every millinery parlor there were three crib houses; for every church there were four gambling halls.

I found a livery for my dun, threw my soogan over my shoulder and headed for the nearest hotel. The winter sun did little to warm the ground. I shivered in my Mackinaw. Despite the cold, dust swirled around my ankles with each step.

The closest hotel was the Dixie, a three-story brick. I had a second-floor room overlooking the street. After freshening up, I found a café and put myself around a meal of beans and tortillas, washed down with warm beer.

The Regulator clock on the wall chimed five as I pushed away from the table and started my search for Hugh Garrett. Outside, the air was growing cooler with the approaching night. I tugged my hat down over my head and turned up the collar of my Mackinaw.

The saloons ranged from fancy establishments with shiny bars imported from the East to adobe huts with dirty canvas hanging from the ceiling to catch falling dirt, spiders, and the occasional snake.

I hit the fancy ones first, remembering Garrett as something of a pompous braggart. Of course, I reminded myself with a chuckle, that description fit most sergeants and corporals I had ever run into, and was usually the reason for losing one or all of their stripes.

I had no luck at any of the establishments. By 2 A.M. I had covered most of the upscale saloons in the downtown area. I was too exhausted to look any further that night.

Next morning, I woke refreshed and ready for the day. After a solid breakfast of meat and potatoes, a pot of coffee, topped off with a slab of apple pie, I headed for the seedier class of saloons.

Midway through the afternoon my persistence paid off. On the outskirts of town at an unnamed adobe saloon with rough planks stretched between two barrels, a Mexican barkeep nodded when I described Garrett. "*Si*, señor. Though it has been many weeks, well I remember that one." He shook his head. "A mean gringo. Me, Luiz Delgado, I was much happy when he leave." Sweat rolled down the fat man's cheeks.

Suppressing my excitement, I asked, "Do you know where he went?"

He shook his head. "Not I, señor."

I glanced around the small room. Three or four *vaqueros* sat in front of the small fireplace, smoking hand-rolled cigarettes and drinking pulque. I pulled out a half eagle. "I'll have some whiskey." He nodded and reached for a bottle on the shelf behind him. While he poured, I asked, "Is there anyone who might know where he went?"

He studied me a moment, and with an indifferent shrug, replied, "When the gringo was here, he spend much time with Maria."

"Maria?"

"*Si*. One of our girls then. This gringo, he spend much time with her."

"I see. And, where can I find her, this Maria?"

He shook his head. "That is not a wise thing to do, señor. Not for a gringo. Maria, she is not one of our girls no more. She has promised herself to Adolfo Rodriguez Pachuca, who is very jealous."

I nodded to the half eagle. "There is more where that came from if I can talk to her."

Greed filled Luiz's eyes as he studied the gold coin on the counter. He looked past my shoulder and called out. "Pablo! Where is your cousin?"

A middle-aged Mexican looked up from the mug of pulque he was nursing. He shrugged. "Who knows where he is. Ask Galeno."

Nodding slowly, Delgado looked up at me slyly. "Me, Luiz Delgado, I can find her for you. Where will you be?"

"At the Dixie Hotel. Room Two-one-four. My name is Thornton."

A sly smile played over his thick lips. His black eyes gleamed. "I will bring her to you, señor."

"Make it fast. I'm pulling out in the morning." I had no plans to leave, but aware of the *mañana* mind-set of most Mexicans I guessed that might speed him up.

Luiz Delgado kept his word. Two hours later, I answered a knock at my door. I opened it to see Delgado and a winsome young senorita facing me.

I invited them in.

Maria looked to be about seventeen, maybe eighteen. She possessed intriguing beauty and grace, from her smooth complexion and striking black eyes to the lithe movements of her slender body.

She nodded when I questioned her. "*Si*. Garrett, he go to Phoenix, but," she added boastfully, "he promise to come back to me. He says he will take me to California."

I glanced at Delgado, puzzled because he had said she was promised to Adolfo Pachuca. Suddenly, I didn't know just how much faith I should put in her words. "*Cuán hace mucho tiempo?* How long ago?"

She shrugged. Her forehead knit in a frown.

Luiz spoke up. "Many weeks, just after the Festival of St. Simon."

Maria nodded and counted her fingers. "Si, it was *siete*, seven weeks ago the festival, it end."

Delgado smiled smugly. "I did as I promise, *si, señor?*"

With a chuckle, I grinned with satisfaction and flipped him a gold eagle. I was drawing closer. "*Si, compadre.* You did as you promised."

Moments after I closed the door behind them, I heard a commotion down the hall. I peeked out and spotted a Mexican *vaquero* wearing a gaudily decorated sombrero, his face dark with anger, raging at Delgado and Maria at the top of the stairs.

He jerked around and glared murderously at me, then seized Maria roughly by her arm and dragged her after him down the stairs. Delgado remained behind, sweating profusely.

I approached. "Trouble?"

Delgado looked up at me. He dragged the tip of his

tongue over his fat lips. "*Si*, señor. Adolfo, he was very angry that Maria, she come to visit you. He thinks you, a gringo, you pay her for her favors."

I stared at him in disbelief. "Didn't you tell him he was wrong, that all I wanted was information?"

The rotund little Mexican nodded emphatically. "*Si, si,* señor. I tell him, but Adolfo, he is very *sospechoso*, how you say, suspicious. I do not think he believed me." He cast a worried glance down the stairs. "I think you must be very careful, señor. It is very difficult to know what Adolfo will do when he is so much angry."

Chapter Nine

I didn't know just how much trust I should have placed on the fat little man's warning. In my drifting over the years, I had met folks of just about every nature and race, from the Chinese working on the railroad up in Utah Territory to black slaves in Virginia. The Mexican hombre was no different. Any of them could turn hot-headed and unreasonable given the right circumstance.

Not knowing Adolfo, I had no idea if Maria's visit to me was enough to set him off, so when I took my supper down in the dining room I made sure I was out of sight from the street and that I had a good view of all doors.

The Dixie Hotel did its best to serve meals with fancy names like Gratinee de Coquilles St. Jacques or Filet mignon aux Oignons. I knew what filet mignon was but

I didn't want to take a chance on that oignons part, so I fell back on my steak and potatoes topped off with apple pie. Traditional and routine I suppose but at least I knew what I was getting.

After supper I settled my account with the hotel, sent word to the livery to saddle my dun and gathered my plunder. I reckoned on moving out. No sense in waiting to see what trouble Adolfo would stir up, if any.

I glanced up at the sky when I started across the street to the livery. A good night for riding—clear skies, a waning moon rising above the Catalina Mountains to the east.

The chill of the night kept many of the townspeople inside. Only a handful were on the street. I rolled my shoulders, enjoying the warmth of my wool Mackinaw in the crisp air.

The pale glow from the barn lantern shone through the open door, laying out a rectangle of light on the ground. I heard my dun snort and whinny softly. "Easy, fella," I called out. "You're going to get plenty exercise, just you—"

When I stepped through the door into the livery I jerked to a halt. Crouched before me in an attack stance, his teeth bared in a savage grimace and his fingers clutching a stiletto blade, Adolfo Rodriguez Pachuca glared at me.

"Now, I will see what the gringo had for supper."

The old livery owner cowered back in one of the stalls.

I stared at the *vaquero* whose black eyes blazed with hate. I remained motionless, my soogan under one arm, my other hand holding the muzzle of my Yellowboy Henry, the butt of which rested on my shoulder.

Adolfo was about my size. He jabbed the needle-like point of his stiletto in my direction. "Prepare yourself, gringo. I will cut your ears from your gringo head and stuff them in your gringo mouth."

I struggled to control my temper. I had gone out of my way to avoid a confrontation but now Adolfo was forcing the issue. Without moving, I replied, "You talk mighty big for a greaser." I figured the demeaning word would set him off.

It did.

With a savage howl he leaped at me, but even as he did I swung the Henry like a club and smashed him just above his temple. He hit the ground unconscious and didn't move a muscle.

The old man crept from the stall and stared down at the unconscious man in disbelief. "Is he . . . is he dead?"

I tied my soogan behind the cantle of my center fire rig and slipped the Henry in the boot. With as much nonchalance as I could muster, I replied, "Got no idea," I swung into the saddle. "None whatsoever."

Heading north out of Tucson I traveled most of the night, pulling off the well-traveled road a spell before the moon dropped below the horizon. By its pale light, I found a dry arroyo, the banks of which were thick with mesquite and ocotillo. Hobbling my dun, I rolled out my soogan on the sandy bed of the arroyo and instantly fell asleep.

Two days later I rode into Phoenix, only to learn after three days of searching that Garrett had ridden out for Prescott, a small town and the former capitol of the territory, three or four days to the north.

A new mine had opened south of Prescott in a place called Skull Valley. Garrett, according to the faro dealer at the Golden Dollar Saloon in Phoenix, had talked about applying for a job to get him through the winter.

I remained composed as I listened to the dealer, but when I left the Golden Dollar there was a new bounce in my step.

While the weather was chilly it was tolerable, but I knew the farther north I rode into the higher elevations my chances of encountering right unpleasant weather were growing faster than a card shark's bank balance.

Two days later as I drew closer to Prescott, I began noticing patches of snow lingering in shady nooks, at the base of boulders, in the corners and bends of various mountain streams, around the bases of the tall pines that surrounded the small village, and under the yellow patches of quaking aspen dotting the countryside.

Prescott was a bustling little community, having served as the capitol of the territory until the previous year when the capitol was moved to Tucson.

By the time I stabled my pony, the sun teetered on

the tips of the pines to the west, and the air carried a frigid edge, sharp enough to cut a jasper's breath.

I shivered as I hurried across the muddy street to a brightly lit saloon, the Nugget, where a blast of warm air with the smell of stale beer and cigarette smoke enveloped me, driving away the shivers.

At the bar I ordered a drink, downed it in one gulp, then ordered another. I leaned back against the bar and sighed. In one corner of the brightly lit saloon, several cowpokes and a handful of hurdy-gurdy girls were gathered around a small tree covered with different colored garlands, and they were joyfully singing "God Rest You Merry Gentleman."

I glanced over my shoulder at the bartender, a baldheaded gent with an amiable grin on his round face. "What's going on over there?"

He laughed. "Where you been keeping yourself, cowboy? It's almost Christmas. Another week."

"I know that, but what's that tree?"

"Oh, that." He laughed again, a broad rollicking laugh. "That came from one of the mine owners. He's a Dutchman, and it seems that back in his country they decorate trees like that to celebrate Christmas." He paused and nodded with twinkling eyes. "Not a bad idea either, huh? Don't know why I never thought of doing it here."

It was obvious the small group was enjoying itself. I grinned. "No, sir, I don't reckon it is a bad idea. Not one bit." And I found myself wondering if Lucy Coulter had put up a tree for Ben and Callie.

One of the girls spotted me, and with a bright smile invited me over. "We need another bass," she laughed.

I downed my drink right fast and poured another. "I don't know if I'm a bass or not, but I never turn down a good songfest."

We broke into "The First Noel," then gave "What Child Is This" a try, but no one knew more than the first couple lines. But it was no matter. We sang the only two carols we knew over and over, and had a fine time doing it.

Next morning, I was going to give myself a good cussing for paying more attention to our caroling, and not enough to those cowpokes coming and going from the saloon.

The saloon also rented out rooms. During the night, a light snow fell, covering the countryside. When I woke, I ambled downstairs for a steaming cup of coffee and a pile of flapjacks with blackstrap molasses.

The room was empty except for two saloon girls in house robes at one table sipping coffee, and the bartender at another. He looked up from his breakfast table and motioned me over. "Might as well join me, cowboy. We got fried eggs and ham this morning with fresh baked bread and sorghum syrup. Coffee's there on the bar."

"Sounds fine to me." I reached for the pot.

"Sue Ann, how about dishing our paying customer up a solid breakfast?"

One of the girls rose and smiled at me. "Coming right up."

I recognized her from the singsong the previous night. I sipped the coffee. This was a right friendly little town.

When I slid in at the table, the bartender extended a hand the size of a ham. "Name's Otto Herman. I own this place."

"Good to meet you. I'm JC Thornton."

At that moment, Sue Ann slid a platter heaped with four fried eggs, a slab of ham the size of Otto's hand, and two wedges of steamy hot bread twice the size of the ham. "Good luck, cowboy," she said with a laugh.

I whistled softly. "Reckon I might need it, ma'am."

After Otto wiped his plate clean, he leaned back, lit a cigar, and sipped his coffee. "Traveling through or looking for work, Thornton? Mines around here are hiring. Always looking for good men."

I don't know if I were just tired of my own cooking, or if it were the altitude, or a combination of both, but that was the best grub I had put myself around for as long as I could remember. Around a mouthful of it, I replied, "Looking for a gent." From under my eyebrows, I saw Otto stiffen slightly. Keeping my eyes on my plate, I added, "Lawyer hired me to find him. The old boy come into a good-sized spread back in Texas. If I can't find him or he turns up deader than a can of corned beef, a second cousin gets the whole shebang."

Otto relaxed. "What's his name?"

Poking another mouthful of grub down my gullet, I replied offhanded, "Garrett. Hugh Garrett."

He pondered the name several moments before shaking his head slowly. "Don't recollect no one by that name around here. And I know most of them. We got half a dozen or so saloons in town here and the boys don't play favorites all that much. Still, wouldn't hurt if you ask the other owners."

I nodded and washed a chunk of bread down with a gulp of coffee. "He might not be using that name. He got accused of some trouble a good while back and left the state. Since then, the law caught the real owlhoots. Old Hugh is free as a song bird." I sipped my coffee again. "He's a couple inches shorter than me. He's got a big round jaw, and his eyes are real close together."

Otto pursed his lips. "I tell you, Thornton. That sounds like Jess McInnis. New in town. Works at the Veigle Mine out at Skull Valley. Comes in pretty regular." He called to the girls. "Sue Ann, have you or Mandy seen Jess McInnis in the last couple days?"

Sue Ann shook her head, but Mandy nodded enthusiastically. "Why, he was in here last night." Her smile faded. "Odd, but he come in, watched the singing for a minute, then just up and left, real fast like he'd forgotten something."

I grimaced inwardly. Garrett had forgotten nothing. When he entered the saloon the night before he must have spotted me. I covered my disappointment with a wry shake of my head. "Just my luck. Now I'll have to run him down at his place. He live around here?" I laid my knife and fork across my empty plate.

"He stays at the bunkhouse at the mine with the other workers at Skull Valley," Sue Ann said.

Taking care not to appear too anxious, I patted my full stomach. "Fine victuals, Otto. Best I've had in quite a spell. You keep serving grub like this, I might just have to settle in this little town of yours."

He laughed. "Navaho squaw does the cooking. Been here ever since I opened up back in sixty-four just after the town got its name from some jasper named Prescott. Since then it has been called Goodwin City and Granite."

"Don't forget Gimletville," Sue Ann put it.

"Or Fleuryville," Mandy added.

I laughed. "Quite a heap of names."

"Reckon so," Otto replied. "But we are growing."

I pushed back from the table. "Well, if you'll give me directions, I reckon I'll ride out to Skull Valley. See if this McInnis jasper is really Garrett. Sure make my life easier."

According to the foreman at the Veigle Mine, McInnis never came back to his bunk the night before. "Yep, he wasn't on the wagon what brought the boys back in from town. Nobody knows what happened. He just didn't show up when it was time to come back. Reckon he got hisself hurt or kilt. That happens a heap. All of his belongings is still at his bunk." He shook his head. "Good worker but he never made no friends. I can't recollect ever seeing him say more than one or two words to nobody."

Chapter Ten

Throughout the entire ride back into Prescott, I called myself every kind of name I could think of. I should have been paying attention to my real task, that of running down Garrett, instead of singing Christmas carols and drinking good whiskey.

I lied to Otto, telling him McInnis was not the man for whom I was searching. "So I reckon I best be riding on."

Otto shook his head. "Don't know if that's too wise, Thornton." He nodded to his kitchen. "That Navaho cook of mine says there's 'heap big snow' coming. Maybe you best hang around until it clears."

I glanced at the sun shining through the window. "I'm not one of the smartest hombres around, Otto, so

I reckon I'll head out. I can pick a few miles before dark."

He arched a skeptical eyebrow. "Good luck."

Swinging into the saddle, I decided to head north instead of backtracking. And then I remembered the words the foreman had spoken. "Yep, he wasn't on the wagon what brought the boys back in from town. Nobody knows what happened. He just didn't show up when it was time to come back."

If Garrett rode in on the wagon, then he had to have a horse to get out of town. I swung by the livery where for the first time in a spell I had a stroke of luck. "Yep," the old man said. "Old boy come in last night, bought a horse and rig—didn't haggle on the price." He shook his head. "Reckon I should have asked more, but anyways he didn't argue none."

"He say where he was going?"

"Not exactly, but asked how far it was to Flagstaff."

I reined around. "Thanks."

"You riding out that way too?"

"Reckon so."

He shook his head, brows knit over his phlegmy eyes. "Got some bad weather coming. Reckon that's a long piece to fight off the cold."

I kept the dun in a running two-step, a mile-eating gait most of the afternoon, but as the winter day waned the clouds began moving in. The wind began its mournful moaning across the prairie of ocotillo and saguaros. The winding road I was following had descended all afternoon. About an hour before sunset, the road began curving and twisting up a slope blanketed by stately pine and spruce, the tips of which seemed to tickle the sagging bellies of the gray clouds scudding past. I figured I had covered about a third of the distance to Flagstaff.

I glanced at the thickening clouds. If the storm held for another twenty-four to thirty-six hours I could outrun it.

Without warning, feathery flakes of snow began to fall. I muttered a soft curse. The night would be darker than the insides of a black bear so I had to make camp while there was still light to see. "Let's look for a cave, fella," I muttered to the dun. "Get us both out of the weather."

The ascending road was a series of switchbacks, the easiest means of climbing steep slopes. Each switchback was about fifty feet above the previous, the slopes between partially covered with talus from the construction of the road. Ahead, I spotted a cave around which talus had fallen, one that appeared large enough for my dun.

The wind picked up, skittering leaves along the hard-packed road.

I glanced over my shoulder at the setting sun. Later, I would reflect that that movement saved my life, for no sooner had I turned than a powerful blow struck my forehead, knocking me from the saddle and spilling me over the edge of road.

Before I opened my eyes, I became aware of wood smoke mixed with the sharp odor of pine needles, and then I smelled the faint but rich aroma of hominy, an aroma from my youth with the Kiowa. With that awareness, I heard voices, garbled and distant. From time to time, damp compresses touched my face, and a stiff crust tugged at the skin on my forehead. And then I felt myself slipping back into darkness.

Slowly, voices began to penetrate the cocoon of silence about me, and familiar odors enveloped me once again. I opened my eyes and stared at the swaying shadows cast by a small fire on the rocky ceiling above my head. A sudden throbbing in my head made me grimace.

A soft voice cut through the silence. "He is awake."

From what seemed a great distance, a booming voice said, "Reckon it's about time. Three days now. Good thing that jasper's got a hard head."

A thick-bearded face with twinkling eyes grinned down at me. "Welcome to the living, friend. How do you feel?"

I blinked against the throbbing pain in my head and mumbled, "Afraid I might live."

He roared. "Glad to hear that. For a spell there I didn't

know if that bullet had scrambled your brains or not." He glanced over his shoulder. "*Alimento, por favor.*"

At the mention of food my stomach growled, overriding the pain in my head.

Moments later, an Indian woman handed the big man a wooden bowl from which tendrils of steam rose. With a spoon twice the size of a white man's spoon, he dipped it in the stew and touched it to my lips. "Hominy and venison. Not too fancy, but it'll stick to your ribs."

While he spoon-fed me, he introduced himself. "Name's Joshua Adams. This here lovely lady is my missus, Yellow Flower, daughter of the Navaho chieftain, Manuelito."

"Thornton," I mumbled between mouthfuls of stew. "JC."

Adams laughed. "Well, JC, reckon you best thank your lucky stars that Yellow Flower there has got such good ears. Three days ago, just as the storm come in, she heard a gunshot. I found you all laid out on a pile of rocks. You'd of certain be nothing but a chunk of ice by now."

I nodded weakly, full and as comfortable as I could be with a head that felt like someone was inside trying to break out with a twelve-pound sledgehammer.

When I next awakened, I looked around the cave. My head felt better. I touched a finger to my forehead and felt a knot the size of a hen egg. Another half inch, I told myself, you wouldn't have a forehead to have a knot on.

Yellow Flower was kneeling by the fire grinding corn. When she heard me stir, she looked around, then quickly rose and disappeared beyond a heavy bearskin draped across the mouth of the cave.

Moments later, Adams returned, shaking the snow off the heavy fur coat about his massive torso. He pulled a floppy sombrero from his head as he ducked through the bearskin door. "Well now," he bellowed. "You look a heap better this morning. Looks like you ain't ready to stumble down that stairway to Hades yet."

He gestured to a neatly stacked pile of clothing at the foot of my bed, which was simply heavy fur hides over a pile of pine boughs. "There's your duds. Yellow Flower, she washed them up good and clean. Think you're strong enough to get up?"

I nodded briefly, not wanting to aggravate my head.

"Good." He hooked his thumb over his shoulder at the hanging bearskin. "Get yourself proper then come on in. Coffee's on, and we got hot corncakes."

To my surprise, when I stepped through the bearskin door, I stepped into a large log cabin. At one end, a fire blazed in a rock fireplace. At the other end, three ponies stood staring at me from behind a pole railing.

Adams looked up from a hand-hewn table. "Come on in and have a seat. What we got ain't fancy, but it's sure plentiful."

With the corncakes was a bowl of mountain honey, johnnycakes, a platter of eight-inch brook trout, gutted, and fried whole and crisp.

"Yellow Flower trapped them yesterday. Figured you might like something special."

I nodded to her. "Much obliged, ma'am."

Adams daubed his trout in the honey and bit off the head. "So, you know something about the Kiowa, huh?"

I almost choked on the coffee. "What?"

He shrugged. "You mumbled in your sleep about Skywalker and Satanta. Kiowa war chiefs. I heard of them from over Texas way."

With a wry grin, I said, "I'm almost afraid to ask what else I might have said."

Adams laughed, and his wife smiled demurely. "Nothing bad, JC. Nothing bad."

During the meal, I told him about my years with the Kiowa. I never cared to reveal much of my life, my dreams to others, but I knew I needed Adams' help to continue my journey on to Flagstaff. So, when he asked where I was heading, I told him where and why.

His face growing hard, the muscular man asked, "You figure he's the jasper what shot you?"

"I don't know who else. He spotted me in Prescott and then hightailed it for Flagstaff. I figured his pony went lame or broke a leg or something, and he waited for some unsuspecting gent to saunter by." With a wry grin, I shook my head. "That unsuspecting gent just happened to be me."

Adams eyed me shrewdly. "I reckon you'd be mighty anxious to track that jasper down, huh?"

"As soon as I can."

He grunted. "JC, you got yourself one chance to get out of here before the snow sets in good and proper. Yellow Flower here figures another storm will hit in two or three days. We'll be stuck right here until spring." He studied me, a frown on his craggy face. "I don't know if you're strong enough to make it or not but you're welcome to one of my ponies and gear. It's an all day and night ride straight through to Flagstaff. Tough even for a woolly bear like me." His frown deepened. "I don't know if that blow to your head addled you or not. It don't appear like it did, but then you ain't gone out and pushed yourself either. You're welcome to winter here with us, but if you're all fired set on running that jasper down, you'd be smart to light a shuck out of here within the hour."

I rose to my feet. For a moment, I swayed unsteadily, but then my head stopped swimming. "Reckon I'll move on then." I jammed my hand in my pocket. "How much for your pony?"

The mountain man shook his head. "You sure you're up to the journey? It'll be mighty rugged."

I forced a grin. "I got no choice. Now, what about the pony?"

"It's yours. Didn't cost me nothing. Used to belong to an Apache brave, but I found him dead and the horse standing by his side. Besides, what with winter coming on, that gives me one less animal to feed."

"Thanks."

He nodded to a heavy bearskin coat. "That coat of

yours got ripped up in the fall you took. Take this one. Keep you warmer than if you was in your mama's arms."

I shook my head but he insisted. "I got me another one."

"Well, thanks again."

I went back into the cave for my hat and sidearm. While there, I stuck two double eagles under my bearskin blanket. Adams would probably cuss me when he found them but if he was the kind of woolly bear I figured, he'd just chuckle and drop them in his pocket.

Chapter Eleven

The Apache pony was a long-haired grulla, a grayish-blue gelding with black points. "He's a stayer from what I've seen." Adams laughed and laid his hand on the worn saddle. With a frosty breath, he said, "Wish I had a better saddle than that stick you're forking there but it'll have to do."

I grinned. "Got no choice." I patted the saddlebags Yellow Flower had packed with grub and extended my hand to Adams. "Obliged to both of you."

He gestured to the saddlebags. "Yellow Flower packed a few petals of peyote in case that noggin of yours starts hurting."

I glanced at her and she turned her eyes away. "Thank you." I nodded to Adams. "Doubt if I'll ever be back this way but you're good people." I offered him my hand. "Been a privilege to know you."

Adams shook my hand, nodded, and stepped back. I reined around and headed up the road. He called after me. "Remember! Keep riding if you want to beat the storm."

Yellow Flower had predicted a cloudless night. I glanced into the clear blue sky and spotted the waning moon to the east. At least I would have a few hours of moonlight.

The night was bright, the air frosty and crisp. After a couple of hours my head began to throb. I pulled out a small parfleche bag and fished a petal of peyote from it. I chewed it up and washed it down with cool water from Adams' canteen.

The grulla proved to be a fine animal. The miles fell behind. My head grew clear with the frigid air. A few hours before sunrise I hit the base of the Mogollon Mesa. The precipitous trail to the rim was a series of switchbacks climbing almost a thousand feet.

With the rising sun I topped out on the Mogollon Rim. Off to the north, a bank of clouds eased over the horizon. Half a mile down the road, smoke rose from the chimney of a trading post.

While downing a cup of thick, black coffee, I listened as the old trader shook his head and told me he had not seen the hombre I described. "Could be he come by at night and just kept right on riding," he added.

I thanked him and swung back in the saddle. Flagstaff was still half a day's ride, and the dark clouds were beginning to roll over the waving tops of the tall pines that spread across the Mogollon Mesa.

The storm hit three hours later.

By the time I rode into Flagstaff, a blizzard was raging. The owner of the livery was nowhere around so I stabled the grulla and placed a gold coin on the stall rail. I'd come back later and settle my bill with him. I glanced around the dark livery, muttering a curse when I failed to spot my dun.

Outside, I had to squint against the blowing snow while turning my shoulder into the wind and struggling up the boardwalk to the closest hotel, The San Francisco Peaks, named after the two mountains directly north of the small town.

In the hotel, Christmas carols echoed through the lobby. A dozen or so folks were gathered around a piano, singing lustily, unwilling to let the storm dampen their spirits.

I was exhausted. When I flopped down on the bed in my room I figured on a short rest, a bite to eat, and then a visit back to the livery. I was asleep before the first bedspring stopped squeaking.

I didn't wake up until the next morning with the blizzard still howling outside. After breakfast, I headed back to the livery to check on the grulla.

A grizzled old man with a gimpy leg grinned toothlessly when he saw me and shifted the wad of tobacco in his mouth from one cheek to the other. "You must be the stranger what left the grulla." He patted his pocket. "Found your money." He gestured to a small room. "Coffee?"

"Why not?" I started for the office and jerked to a halt, my eyes on a dun on the far side of the livery. I looked back at the old man. "That dun over there. Where'd you get him?"

A frown deepened the wrinkles on the old man's forehead and the affable smile faded from his face. "What business do it be of yours, mister?"

"Because the dun belongs to me." I touched the scab on my forehead. "The jasper that rode in on it did this to me."

The light of understanding lit his eyes. "So that's what it was." He shifted the wad of tobacco from one side of his jaw to the other.

"What do you mean, that's what it was?"

He twisted his lips from one side to the other. "Three or four days back, this jasper come boiling in like his tail was on fire. Bought a six-year-old dapple gray and rode straight out, heading east." He removed his battered hat and scratched his thinning gray hair. "I reckoned it was mighty peculiar like." He pointed to the corral gate.

"Yep, I stood right there and watched him ride out of town."

I knew he was talking about Garrett but I had to make sure. "You remember what he looked like?"

"Reckon so." He loosed a stream of tobacco on the ground and pointed two fingers at his eyes. "Eyes real close together. Never seen no one's that close. Kinda snake-like."

Frustrated, I stared out the door at the raging blizzard. Three days. No telling where he was now.

The blizzard unleashed its fury on the town for two more days, keeping everyone inside.

During those two days, when I wasn't trying to figure out where Garrett might have gone, I was thinking about the Coulters back in Texas, wondering how they were handling their first winter away from Virginia.

Of course, the truth was, I was thinking more about Lucy Coulter than her husband. I chided myself for such thoughts but I couldn't help them.

Back to Garrett. I figured Santa Fe was snowed in, so that meant Garrett was probably headed south for Mesilla, just north of El Paso.

On the third day, the sun rose in a clear sky, its glare shattered into millions of diamonds by the pristine snow. Travel was impossible. I kept a keen eye on the weather, hoping for enough melt so I could push out for Mesilla.

That night in one of the local saloons I overhead two

rawhide-clad hombres at the table behind me discussing the best route to El Paso, Texas.

I had also been pondering the route back. I wanted to cut southeast, slice across the territory and hit Mesilla at the Rio Grande River in southern New Mexico Territory, but for a single traveler such a route was certain death. My best bet, I had decided, was the backtrack over the heavier traveled roads to Phoenix and Tucson, and then across the El Paso, a route that would take three or four weeks longer than the one to Mesilla.

"Excuse me, gents," I said, scooting around in my chair and facing them. On the table between the two hard-looking hombres lay two big Sharps. The rifles looked to be the big .45/120/550s. Buffalo hunters, I figured. "I couldn't help hear you palavering about El Paso. You don't mind, I'd like to talk to you about it. You see, I'm interested in getting down there without wasting a heap of time."

They eyed me suspiciously. One growled, "We're listening."

Two days later, Caleb Harper, Luke Sowell and I pulled out of Flagstaff, each on a sound pony with two pack animals behind us. With our firepower, we would prove to be a formidable foe for any wandering war party.

Chapter Twelve

W e headed southeast, dropping down into lower country. A week out we had our first encounter with Indians when three Comanche approached our noon fire with upheld palms, signifying friendship.

We shared our bacon and coffee with them, and after a short visit, during which they quickly took in our weapons, they rode out over our back trail.

Two or three times in the next few weeks we spotted small bands of Indians, but the Comanche word of our firepower and the winter weather permitted us to ride into Mesilla without incident.

Garrett had vanished. No one in Mesilla had seen him. I glanced back to the north and cursed. Somewhere I'd passed up his trail.

But where?

Back to the south were Texas and the Coulters. The urge to travel back to Kimble County was overpowering.

Two days later, I left Caleb and Luke in El Paso and followed the Rio Grande for the next three days to Sierra Vieja Mountains where I cut east for Fort Davis near the Davis Mountains. My only run-in with Indians was a band of Comanche on the western slopes of the mountain range.

Two miles before I reached the foothills, while the sun was still above the western horizon, I built a small, smokeless fire and boiled some coffee. Chewing on dried corncakes and jerky I'd picked up back in El Paso, I washed them down with steaming coffee, and swung back in the saddle as a bank of clouds rolled across the northern horizon.

I hoped the clouds meant only a dry cold front and a dark night. When I started up into the foothills sometime later, I pulled off the trail, searching for a snug little nook for a cold camp in the jumble of granite boulders with a view of the trail.

I grinned when I found exactly what I was looking for. The hidey-hole was horseshoe shaped, and on one end was a small basin of water that drained from a fissure above, running from the basin down into the rocks.

I glanced around, making sure I had a back way out.

The trail out led around several boulders, then down a wash that led to the prairie.

Never having explored the Davis Mountains, I planned on skirting them to the south, coming into Fort Davis from the southwest.

Being the middle of February, the weather remained cold. As much as I wished for a fire, I had camped cold every night out of El Paso. I planned no changes this night. I'd filled my belly earlier, so I had to content myself with jerky and water.

While I had seen nothing in the last few days of which I needed to be concerned, I was well aware that a single, simple mistake could leave my bones bleaching on the prairie.

No sooner had I settled down between the boulders than I heard the click of hooves from below. I glanced at my grulla whose ears were perked forward and whose eyes were focused on the sound. Silently, I rose and gently pinched his nostrils and listened, waiting for the sounds to pass.

The click of hooves stopped. I muttered a soft curse and peered into the darkness below. A small flame appeared. Moments later, another nearby. I made out the lithe forms of Indian braves around the fires.

Their voices drifted faintly up the slope, too faint to understand, but cold fear stabbed my heart when one of the Indians came into the firelight and I recognized the Comanche sign on the pony's chest.

I whispered to the grulla, "Easy, boy. Easy."

Quickly, I cut four squares from my wool blanket and gently tied them around his hooves. Having memorized the twists and turns in my escape trail, I didn't anticipate any problems reaching the prairie below despite the thick shadows.

Suddenly, the feather-soft whisper of leather on rock froze me. We were in the shadows on one end of our hideaway, around the bend from the water. I crouched, peering in the direction of the sound.

It grew louder, and came the gurgling of water filling canteens.

Suddenly, the gurgling ceased, and the faint click on a canteen being laid on rock reached my ears. When I heard the Indian grunt and sniff, I knew he had smelled the grulla. Drawing my Colt, I rose to my feet and leaned up against the granite wall just around the bend from the small basin of water.

I strained to pick up the faint scuff of his moccasins against rock. They drew close, then paused. He sniffed again. I flexed my fingers on the butt of my Colt, hoping the brave was where I thought he was. He shuffled forward once again.

Clenching my teeth, I swung the muzzle of the Colt. It slammed into bone, followed by a small groan, and then the sound of a body hitting the ground.

There came a death rattle from the fallen warrior's throat, and then all was silent. Warily, I laid my hand on his chest. He was dead. I muttered a silent curse.

Without hesitation, I pulled off my neckerchief and tucked it under the bridle to cover the grulla's eyes to assuage his fear, then led him around the bend and along the rear escape route, blindly feeling my way.

Once out of the foothills, I headed south to circle the mountains, hoping to put several miles between me and the Comanche war party before sunrise.

The sun rose on a leaden, threatening sky. I scooted around in my saddle and peered over my back trail. I had reached the southern foothills of the mountain. For a moment, I thought I spotted a cloud of dust. I studied it for several moments, then figured my eyes were playing tricks. I turned east toward Fort Davis.

I guessed I was a half-day's ride from the fort, where I could swap ponies, stock up on grub, and after a night's rest head due east.

I'd heard stories of Fort Davis, which was established fourteen years earlier on the site of an old Indian village, which the early settlers called Painted Comanche Camp. The location was ideal as it was the crossroads from Presidio to San Antonio to El Paso.

With the establishment of the fort, a small village by the name of Chihuahua came into existence southwest of the fort. During the war, the Confederacy deserted the fort, and the year before, in 1867, the Ninth US Cavalry took over. Chihuahua took the name of the fort.

Mid-afternoon I rode in and spent the next hour futilely trying to swap the grulla for another remount, but

none of the animals could begin to match the grulla despite the hard traveling I'd put the gelding through for
the past couple months.

Finally, I gave up in frustration. Seemed like every
horse I saw was bandy-legged, buck-kneed, cow-hocked,
or rubbernecked. All I could do was shake my head in
frustration at the sickle-hocked piebald a toothless old
horse trader tried to put off on me.

So I put the grulla in the livery, paid to have him
rubbed down and grained, and decided to give him a
couple of days' rest before pushing on.

The hotel was a single-storey rock building with a
covered porch. After stashing my plunder in my room,
I got a hot bath and shaved the beard from my face. I
came out feeling ten pounds lighter.

That night, a roaring fire kept the chill at bay, and the
dining area was awash in laughter by teamsters and
stagecoach passengers laying over for the night.

Fort Davis was like many pioneer villages, populated
by various cultures, and creating a racial mix with which
one quickly acclimated. And for most westerners, preju-
dices were forgotten.

That's why I didn't give more than a cursory glance at
the handful of Indians in white man's dress who worked
in various businesses in the small town.

My last night, I sat with a handful of teamsters in
front of a roaring fire, enjoying a cigarette and whiskey
as they informed me of the best route to Kimble County.

Growled one bearded teamster, "Take the San Antone road east. Ten miles out when it cuts south, you head the other direction, back to the north and east. Sometime tomorrow afternoon, you'll run across a faint wagon trail that'll take you straight into Kimble County." I nodded with satisfaction. There would be only a hundred miles or so of country with which I was not familiar.

Next morning I pulled out, the grulla fully rested and tugging at the reins. I had cleaned and oiled my Yellow-boy Henry and my .36 Navy Colt and stocked up on enough cartridges to fight off the entire Nokoni clan of the Comanche.

The day was one of those winter days with a brilliant blue sky and no wind. I put the grulla in a running two-step across the rolling prairie of sage and bunchgrass. From time to time we'd spook jackrabbits or roadrunners. Some zigzagged through the sage to evade us. Others simply stood and watched curiously as we passed, and one or two even decided to race along with us.

An hour out of Fort Davis I spotted dust to the north, but it turned to be a small herd of antelope, those bouncing white–tailed animals that can cover forty feet in a single leap.

Mid-morning, I left the San Antonio road and headed northeast across the prairie. The sky remained clear, the air crisp, and the winter sun baked my shoulders.

Suddenly, my grulla jerked aside and reared, pawing the sky. When he came down, he spun to the left as the frightening chilling buzz of a rattlesnake ripped through the air.

By the time I pulled the grulla under control, the rattler had slithered from the rocks on which he had been sunning and disappeared into a fissure in the ground.

My pony began favoring his front left. I dismounted and checked for fractures in the pastern or fetlock and even in the shank, but there were no broken bones.

From time to time I spotted other puffs of dust. Mid-afternoon, I ran across the wagon trail the old teamster had told me about. With a broad grin on my face, I cut due east, bound for Kimble County.

Thirty minutes later as I topped a rise, I reined up and caught my breath.

Below, grazing calmly, was a herd of hump-backed buffalo was at least a mile across, and probably that from front to rear.

I had planned on reaching the Pecos River that night, but skirting the herd of buffalo took longer than I figured, so I camped in a shallow wash.

During the night I jerked awake, not quite certain just what had awakened me. The grulla was staring off to the north. He stomped his foot and snorted. Crawling to the top of the wash, I peered into the blackness.

In the pale starlight I made out a column of Indians riding east, the same direction I was heading.

I remained motionless, watching until they disappeared, wondering just what was so urgent for them to travel after dark.

During the last two years I spent with the Kiowa, my Indian brother Red Eagle and I rode with three war parties, not to fight, but as jinglers, watching after their ponies at night. During those years as well as the previous four, I never heard of parties traveling at night unless they were hard-pressed to go somewhere.

So why this band?

When false dawn filled the sky, I was still watching and wondering.

I hurried back to my unrolled soogan and quickly put all my plunder together. Before cinching down my saddle, I checked the grulla's leg. I muttered a soft curse and grimaced when I felt a slight spongy swelling about the fetlock and knee. I had hoped he had not strained it the day before when he shied away from the rattler, but obviously he had.

Pushing to my feet, I ran my hand over his neck. "You'll be fine, fella. We'll just take it easy today."

I hoped.

Chapter Thirteen

I continued east, noting smaller herds of buffalo moving slowly northward. Warily studying the lay of the rolling prairie around me, I continued to scan the horizon for clouds of dust. I knew from experience that a single sage bush could hide a crouching brave, that a sprinkling of leaves and tiny branches could cover a warrior crouched in a hole, that a patch of buffalo grass could conceal a prone Koitsenko.

More than one unsuspecting jasper's bones had ended bleaching in the sun because things around him looked normal. In the West, normal wasn't even in the dictionary.

I skirted two or three herds of grazing buffalo, watched by the bull sentries as I passed. I gave them a wide berth, not wanting to spook them and force my grulla into a sudden gallop to evade their charge. So far, he had given no indication his leg was bothering him.

Mid-morning, after detouring around a herd guarded by two or three particularly aggressive sentries, I spotted faint puffs of dust directly in front of me, near where I figured the Pecos River lay.

While my journey from Falls County to Tucson last winter took me farther north, I discovered when I crossed the Pecos River there were only a few safe fords because of the steep, almost perpendicular banks of the river.

At the time, I made a mental note that those crossings offered ideal situations for ambush.

And now as I approached the river, the hair on the back of my neck bristled, and the band of mysterious warriors from the previous night was in the front of my mind.

Reining up, I studied the trail ahead, pondering my situation. I learned early in my years with the Kiowa that when a situation was unknown the smart move is to expect the worse.

I didn't know if this was just a wandering war party out to see what they could find or that band from the Davis Mountains. As far as I knew, after discovering their dead companion, they could have tracked me to Fort Davis, for once I reached the foothills that night I didn't waste time covering my tracks. The Indians at the fort could have given them the direction I had taken.

And I could be blowing in the wind, but I couldn't take a chance. If I rode down to the river all by myself and they were waiting, I'd most likely end up staring at the sky and seeing nothing.

Glancing over my shoulder at the massive sentry bull eyeing me with those beady little eyes, I knew exactly what I was going to do.

With a click of my tongue, I put my grulla in a wide circle around the herd, which I guessed numbered a couple hundred or so. Once on their west side, I reined up and quickly dismounted. Running my hands over the grulla's leg, I grunted with satisfaction. The swelling had subsided some, but I hadn't pushed the animal hard. Now, I was going to demand all the sturdy little pony had, and then probably a tad more. Still squatting by his leg, I drew a deep breath and sighed loudly, saying a short prayer that his leg would hold up.

I swung into the saddle, shucked my Yellowboy Henry from the boot, let out a Rebel yell, fired once into the sky, and dug my spurs into the grulla.

Like a great black blanket, the herd bolted toward the river. I dug my heels in the grulla's flanks, driving the gelding near the lead animals just in case they decided to swerve away from the river.

Like most animals, buffalo follow the path of least resistance, and though faint, the wagon trail to the river was discernable from the surrounding prairie of sage and buffalo grass.

Dust billowed from hundreds of pounding hooves. I

pulled my neckerchief up over my nose and squinted into the thick clouds of sand swirling over the herd.

I continued shouting and firing the Henry, saving the cartridges in my Colt for when we hit the river.

Just before we reached the sloping trail down to the churning waters of the Pecos, I booted the Henry and shucked my Colt, and muttered a hasty prayer that my pony's leg would hold up as we raced down the slope and into the river.

The lead buffaloes were about thirty yards ahead of me. No sooner had they dropped out of sight below the riverbank than a fusillade of gunfire exploded above the thunder of their hooves.

Caught up in the thundering herd as we roared over the edge and down the slope, I spurred my pony and clenched my teeth, firing at the puffs of smoke that appeared in the billowing dust.

Every muscle tense, I remained glued in that saddle, expecting at any moment to feel the shuddering of the grulla's muscles as his leg gave way or the impact of a hot slug.

The lead buffalo hit the shallow ford, sending up a spray of water, then stormed up the far bank. I stayed with them.

Suddenly a figure appeared on the rim. I snapped off a shot, and the figure spun to the ground, but not before I recognized him as Comanche.

Moments later, we hit the rim and the herd veered back to the southeast. I remained with them. Behind, all

I could see was a choking cloud of dust, cutting off the river from view. I grinned. If I couldn't see them, they couldn't see me.

If my luck would just hold. But my grin faded. The Comanche were a vengeful people. Only death could quench the heated blood that drove them to pursue one who had killed their own.

The stampeding herd crested a hill and dropped down into a valley, blocking the river from view. Grunting buffalo thundered on either side of my racing pony. I reined him to the left, at the same time firing a shot in front of the lead buffalo.

A small number of the herd splintered, heading northeast. I stayed with them. One by one, they began to slow and fall off to one side or the other until the last one peeled away. By now I figured I was two or three miles from the river.

Angling northeast, I rode steady for the next week, camping cold, pausing long enough for a nap and to provide a short rest for my grulla. The game little gelding had showed me a heart the size of the Rocky Mountains.

The swelling had gone down in his leg, and despite the hard ride, he was in fair shape, probably better than I was.

Just before sunset, I spotted a familiar landmark, a motte of scrubby mesquite surrounding a jumble of boulders with a spring of fresh water. I reined up, studying it for any sign of movement. I had camped there last October on my way to Arizona Territory.

Best of my recollection, the headwaters of the Llano River were only another day to the east.

I remained where I was, resting my hands on the saddle horn and standing in my stirrups while I closely studied the inviting cluster of trees and rocks.

There was no movement, no sound.

With a click of my tongue, I eased forward. Usually on hot days even around the first of March, birds perched in the shade cast by overhead leaves, but I saw none flittering about.

Still a hundred yards away, I rode in a circle around the spring, reading sign that told me several different specie of animal other than man had visited the spring in the last few days.

Finally, I rode in, but the fact no birds were around still bothered me enough that I hastily built a small fire from dry mesquite for coffee and some jerky stew before darkness fell, then quickly stomped it out. After a spare supper, I rode east another mile before pulling into a small patch of mesquite just beyond a small rise for the night.

As I leaned up against the trunk of a mesquite with my soogan draped around my shoulders and my Colt in my lap, I felt somewhat more secure, at least as secure as a jasper can feel when he's stuck in the middle of nowhere at night with marauding bands of Comanche skulking about.

I awakened well before false dawn next morning. As I tightened the cinch about the grulla's belly, I smelled wood smoke.

Wrapping the reins about a mesquite limb, I crept to the top of the small rise and peered over my back trail. A faint tendril of smoke rose from the spring. I studied it for several moments, knowing instinctively that the fire was not built by white men but Indians. It was too small, and they were too quiet.

Backing away, I swung into the saddle and headed east, keeping the grulla in a walk. Out there on the rolling West Texas prairie, only sage, buffalo grass, thin gramma, and rocks held the ground together, and any pace other than a walk threw up dust.

Once or twice during the morning, I spotted puffs of dust behind. Deliberately, I swung southeast, keeping a close watch over my shoulder. To my relief, I saw no evidence of pursuit.

I couldn't help wondering about the war party, where it was headed. I didn't figure it was the Comanche from the Davis Mountains. My scheme with the stampeding buffalo must have thrown them off my trail. Still, I puzzled over the status of the brave I killed back there by the water hole. He must have been important for them to track me as far as they did.

Throughout the remainder of the day I kept a close

eye on my back trail. While I spied no rising dust I remained wary.

At dusk, I cut due south. When I figured it was midnight according to the Big Dipper, I cut east until the handle of the Dipper indicated 2 A.M., and then I reined the grulla directly for the North Star.

Next morning, I greeted the rising sun with bleary eyes and weary muscles. The grulla didn't feel much better, for the worn-out animal stumbled over the rocky ground from time to time

Reining up on a crest of a sage-covered rise, I searched the country around me all the way to the horizon. Other than a couple of coyotes, one or two hawks, and a rattlesnake, I saw nothing.

Figuring I had at least ten or twelve hours on whoever might be behind, I pulled down into a sandy arroyo for a couple of hours' sleep.

A bad dream came true when I awakened. A painted Comanche warrior was staring down at me.

Chapter Fourteen

I must have surprised the warrior when I opened my eyes for he hesitated momentarily, his war axe over his head. Then with a grunt, he slammed the axe down at my head. I glimpsed a flash of sunlight off the metal as I jerked my head aside and kicked out with my feet, catching him on the knee and knocking his blow off just enough to graze the back of my head.

I rolled to my feet as he caught himself, then charged, his feral teeth bared, his brutish face twisted into grotesque savagery. With a guttural growl he swung the war axe. I leaped aside, grabbing his wrist with both hands and, ducking under his arm the way my Kiowa father had instructed, yanked hard, jerking his torso down and flipping his legs over his head. He slammed to the ground on his back.

Before he could move, I kicked him in the side of the head. His wiry body went limp.

Quickly, I shucked my Colt and looked around. The only sign of life was my grulla staring at us, curious as to the commotion.

I peered over the rim of the arroyo. The prairie was empty, devoid of movement. With a frown, I backtracked the Comanche around a bend and spotted his little gray mustang standing motionless, unperturbed.

Muttering a soft curse, I hurried back to my pony and swung into the saddle. I studied the unconscious Indian and decided not to kill him. Instead, I'd leave him afoot, so I grabbed the mustang's rope and headed east. I had no idea if the Comanche was a member of the band from the Davis Mountains or from another band of marauding renegades.

That night, I reached the headwaters of the Llano River and found a snug, out-of-the way camp with sweet water and young bluestem gramma for the two ponies. The mustang was a sound horse. I had thought about turning him loose after a few miles, but he followed my lead so well I decided to make him a present to Ben. After all, every western boy needs his own horse.

Next morning at the river's edge, I dropped to my belly for a drink of sweet water before riding out. I frowned at my reflection. For a moment, I didn't recognize the long-haired hombre staring back at me. My beard was growing thick, my hair was over my ears, and with the heavy bearskin coat wrapped about me, I looked like I had just come down from a year's beaver trapping up in the Rockies.

Well, I thought, swinging into the saddle, *I'll clean up good and proper when I reach Falls County.*

Two days later, I paused at a creek feeding into the Llano River and let the ponies drink. I wondered if this was the one Coulter called Silver Creek. I sniffed the air. Wood smoke. I peered into the forest of blackjack oak and pignut hickory along the river.

I shucked my Colt .36 and forded the creek, easing along the river's shore. If I remembered right, a mile or so ahead were the ruins of the old cabin I had run across on my trip last autumn.

Around the next bend a half-mile down the river, I jerked to a halt.

There on the crest of the hill sat the old rock cabin, smoke drifting up from its chimney. I gaped in surprise. The cabin had been rebuilt. Just west of it, a pole barn had been erected with a rail corral surrounding it.

Four horses and half a dozen mules stood inside the corral, staring at me. Next to the stone cabin sat a wagon, a prairie schooner, like the kind Floyd Coulter had brought down from Fort Worth.

For a moment, an outrageous idea filled my head, but I quickly discarded it. Holstering my sixgun, I rode ahead, stopping some hundred feet or so from the cabin. "Hello, the cabin!" I shouted.

The slab door burst open and a young boy ran out.

My jaw dropped down to the saddle horn when he called out, "Floyd. There's a stranger out here."

From the corner of my eye, I saw movement from the pole barn. I glanced around as Wishbone ambled up to the corral fence and rested his arms on the opera rail, staring at me curiously.

Coulter stepped onto the porch. "Howdy, stranger. Coffee's hot. You're welcome to come for a spell."

I finally found my voice. "Coulter. It's me. Thornton. JC Thornton."

Coulter's smile faded into a frown while young Ben shouted, "Ma! It's Mr. Thornton! He's back!"

"Thornton? Is that you behind that beard?" Coulter called out.

I grinned. "Sure as shooting."

He waved me in. "Well, you bring yourself in here and let us get a good look at you. We was hoping you'd make it back."

Lucy Coulter stepped through the open door, a smile on her face.

I felt like a young buck of eighteen again. Dismounting, I untied the mustang's lead rope and held it out to Ben. "Here you go, boy. A horse of your own."

Ben's eyes lit. He glanced at his mother who gave him a brief nod. That was all he needed to make a wild dash for the lead rope. "A horse. All my own."

Wishbone had climbed through the rails and was hurrying toward me. Three other jaspers came out of the barn and ambled over.

After a round of greetings, Coulter introduced me to his hired hands Mack Rust, George Wingo, and Nat Gallatin. Rust and Wingo were older hombres, mid-thirties or so, a mite old for hiring out. Wingo, a burly hombre, had a sly look in his eye while Rust seemed, like his handle, just worn out. Gallatin was a young innocent, probably away from home for the first time.

I don't know who had the most questions, me or the Coulters.

After I related my travels over the last five months, Coulter explained how not long after I left a federal troop came through with plans to set up forts in the uninhabited areas of Texas.

When Coulter learned one of the forts was to be on the Llano River, he decided to accompany the troop. His brother, Sam, would come later.

He explained that he'd hired his men there in Alta Springs the day before they pulled out. "A big worry off my mind," he muttered, puffing on his pipe. "I was right concerned about Indians for Lucy and the children's sake, but what with an Army fort only a few miles away, I reckon I can sleep a heap better now."

Later, Wishbone sat on the riverbank while I scraped off my beard and soaped down in the cold waters of the Llano. "Too bad you didn't find Garrett."

"I was close, mighty close." I paused and glanced at the barn. "When did you all get out here?"

"Around the last of November. We got lucky though. I don't know about Arizona, but we had us a right warm spell almost up to Christmas. Mighty cold since then. Anyway, by that time, we had the cabin up and snug, and a small room at the barn to throw our soogans. Miz Coulter, she does all the cooking. We do all the work." He surveyed the country around us. "Coulter's got hisself a nice spread here. Sorta makes me think about getting myself one. Maybe drift down to South Texas and pick up a drive to Kansas, then use my pay to get started."

I slipped into some dry duds I'd borrowed from young Gallatin. I nodded to the barn. "What about Wingo and Rust? They good hands?"

Wishbone shrugged. "Just wintering, I figure. Come spring in another few weeks I reckon they'll light a shuck out of here. The kid, he'll stay. Orphan boy. Fourteen."

I arched an eyebrow. "Big for his age."

With a chuckle, Wishbone replied, "Been in so many orphanages and foster homes, he had to grow up in a hurry." The redheaded cowpoke grew serious. "Glad you're here, JC. I been seeing some Injun sign. Ain't seen none of them but they're about. I'm figuring with spring coming on they'll be moving about."

"At least the fort's close by."

"Such as it is."

Chapter Fifteen

The bunkroom on the side of the pole barn was constructed with logs chinked with mud and grass and with a solid roof that served as a loft to store hay for winter feeding. Four bunks fashioned with small tree trunks sat around the walls. A fireplace warmed the room.

I rolled out my soogan on the floor.

Wingo pulled out some cigarette makings. "You planning on hanging around, Thornton?" There was a hint in his tone that perhaps I should be moving on.

"Hadn't decided. Reckon it depends on Coulter."

Wingo grunted. "Reckon so. Me and Coulter got about all the hands we need for the work we got. Hate to see you give up any plans you might have just to hang around here."

I suppressed a grin. "That's right kindly for you to be

concerned about me. Not too many jaspers today pay much attention to the welfare of others."

Wishbone grinned and rolled his eyes.

Across the room, Rust was snoring, and young Gallatin was reading a newspaper by candlelight. He glanced at me. "You read, Thornton?"

"Some."

He gestured to a box under his bunk. "I got a heap of books and newspapers under here. You're welcome to them"

"Thanks. What's that you're reading now?"

He held it up. "*Illustrated Police News.*" He grinned sheepishly. "Of course, it's about six months old but I still like to read it."

That night as I lay awake staring at the last glimmer of light flickering on the ceiling, I wondered about Wingo. He was a braggard, full of his own self-importance. The others, Rust and Gallatin, they'd do to ride the river with, but Wingo was one of those jaspers who cared about only one person—himself.

Next morning, Coulter and I rode down to the sutler's at the fort to pick up his mail. From the way Wishbone had talked, I was curious to see just how much protection the Coulters could expect when Indian trouble arose, and arise it would.

My buffalo hunting companions with whom I'd journeyed through Arizona and New Mexico Territory had talked often about the unrest among the Comanche, so I had no reason not to expect it.

Fort Kimble was a series of log cabins constructed around three sides of a quadrangle a couple acres square. Behind the cabins on one side of the quadrangle was a corral with a long pole barn on one side.

The fourth side of the quadrangle was the civilian side with a saloon, The Kimble Emporium, a blacksmith, and the sulter's. The store was a combination military commissary and general store with everything from barrels of flour to spanking new Winchester 66s.

Upon leaving the sulter's, we ran into the post commander, Captain Charles L Irwin, from Philadelphia, Pennsylvania. He was an amiable gent with no idea about how to fight the Indian, having been steeped in military strategy utilized by the federal Army during the recent War of Secession. His tactics, carryovers from the Revolutionary War, would make Comanche chiefs like Buffalo Hump and Quanah Parker laugh.

During the ride back to the ranch, I asked Coulter about Rust and Wingo.

"Reckon they pull their weight. Now, Nat, he's a worker, but them other two . . . well, truth is, they was the only able-bodied jaspers who took me up on my job offer. Still, I can't complain none, for we've done a heap more than I reckoned we would."

We fell silent. From time to time, Coulter glanced at

me. I knew he had something on his mind. Finally, he cleared his throat. "What are your plans, Thornton? Now, they ain't none of my business, but the reason I'm asking is that I'd like for you to stay on."

I grinned wryly. "Seems like you got more hands than you need right now."

"Maybe so, but I figure Wingo and Rust is going to light a shuck out soon as the weather warms." He shrugged. "I might be wrong but they never struck me as the staying type."

I scooted around in the saddle and looked at him. "I'm obliged for the offer, but understand, I'm looking for Garrett. I could be gone tomorrow."

He nodded. "I know that. That don't bother me if it don't you."

Wingo sulled up when he learned I was rolling out my soogan permanent-like. That night in the bunkhouse, he tapped me on the shoulder. I turned to face him. A couple inches taller than me and fifty pounds heavier, he glared down at me. "I thought you was riding on out, Thornton?"

The brusque tone caused the other three cowhands to stop what they were doing and turn their attention on us. Tension crackled through the small room.

With a faint smile, I studied him. "Reckon I changed my mind."

He flexed and unflexed his fists. His eyes burned into

mine, and I could tell he was spoiling for a fight, but what puzzled me was that if he was looking for one, why didn't he get on with it?

"I told you we had no work for you." His eyes narrowed as if daring me to dispute his word.

My smile grew wider. "Then either you or Floyd Coulter are wrong. Were I you, I'd be sure I was right before I started talking."

By now, the larger man was almost trembling. With an angry curse, he turned on his heel and stomped from the bunkhouse.

Sighs of relief broke the silence.

Wishbone touched a match to the cigarette he had been building. "Best watch that one, JC," he whispered under his breath. "He'll come at you from the back."

I shook my head, still puzzled. "If I ever seen someone spoiling for a fight, he is."

Wishbone chuckled. "Sure is, ain't he?"

The tone of his voice hinted he knew more than he had told me. "What's going on?"

The redheaded cowpoke grinned. "I told him how you cleaned out them saloons in Wichita and Dodge." His grin faded. "Wingo's a coward. He ain't going to fight no one he figures can whip him. That's why I say, look out for your back."

Spring came early, and we were all caught up in building Floyd Coulter's ranch.

Wingo never said more to me than he had to, but I knew if I got snake bit, he'd be the last one to volunteer to suck out the poison.

Little Ben would have stayed on that Comanche mustang ten, twelve hours a day if his ma had let him. Still, what few hours he could manage, he caught on fast.

Lucy Coulter didn't change. She was sturdy, patient, considerate, and still one of the most fetching ladies I had ever met. More than once at night, I drifted off thinking about her, only to awaken next morning ashamed of myself.

To my surprise, we encountered no problems with Indian intrusions.

For the first time since my court-martial, I found myself enjoying life.

From time to time, footloose cowpokes bound for San Antonio or Harrisburg drifted past, shared a meal, and rolled their blankets on the floor in front of the fireplace.

It was from one of those jaspers that I learned Hugh Garrett was running a saloon in Santa Fe.

Next morning before the sun rose, I pulled out, but not before Wishbone, young Gallatin, and the Coulters cautioned me to take care. Lucy laid her hand on mine and whispered, "You're a good man, JC Thornton. Come back to us."

Truth is, I almost decided to forget about Hugh Garrett right then, but I had no choice. I had to go, but in the weeks ahead, in those days when it seemed there was no way out, her words kept me going.

Chapter Sixteen

Riding straight through to Santa Fe took up about twenty days, but dodging Comanche war parties, Comancheros, and renegades added another three weeks to my trip.

According to my calculations, it was the last week in April when I topped the crest of a ridge of the Sangre de Cristo Mountains and looked down on Santa Fe. Instead of the small city clinging to the slope on the far ridge I had seen years earlier, it now covered the entire slope, disappearing over the crest of the ridge. The village I had ridden through years past had changed considerably from a sleepy pueblo to a thriving market where the crossroads of the country converged.

For several minutes, I sat gazing down on the sprawling city of adobe, where striking red-tile roofs contrasted sharply with the dazzling whitewashed buildings. Knowing if Garrett spotted me, he would run like a rabbit, I had let my beard and hair grow.

While I still had no idea just what I would do to force the truth from Garrett, I concerned myself with first running him down. Then I would worry about the next step.

I could tell from my perch on the ridge above the bustling city that my task would not be easy. With dozens of freight lines pushing in from every direction of the compass, it would be a toss-up as to which there were more of, saloons or crib houses.

My funds were running low. I managed to land a job in a livery for ten dollars a month. The job was the kind that rendered an individual invisible, which was fine with me. On top of that, I could roll out my soogan on the hay up in the loft.

The livery owner, Enrico Mio Salazar, had his fat finger in dozens of enterprises throughout the city, many legitimate, but just as many illegal. Before hiring me, he studied me intently, trying to figure just what kind of gringo would be willing to work for a Mexican.

"I hold no argument against any people," I told him. "The only ones I hold grudge against are those who try to tell me what to do." I knew, given the pride inherent in his culture, that he would understand my intent.

He grinned and snapped his fingers for his carriage.

"*Si*, Thornton. We understand each other." He gestured to the livery. "I send *los mensajeros* each evening to pick up *los ingresos*, the income, of the day."

I nodded. "I'll be expecting them."

And the truth was, he was a good boss. As long as I turned the day's profits over to his couriers, he left me alone.

In a strange city, questions could get back to the wrong people so I made it a point to ask none, only to observe. In my spare time, I methodically covered the city, barrio by barrio, making six or seven saloons whenever I could take breaks from the livery.

From time to time, federal troops rode past, and I learned there was a sizable federal outpost several miles north of the city.

Three weeks passed, and I was still no closer to Hugh Garrett than when I first rode into Santa Fe. The days were growing warmer, although ice still rimmed small pools of water each morning.

With the coming of warmer weather, I made another foolish decision to take off my beard. I had just finished scraping off the last of the coarse whiskers when a well-dressed *caballero* rode in on a magnificent black stallion. He took in the livery in a glance. He was dressed in the aristocratic taste of a *hidalgo*, the Spanish upper class, with a flat-crowned, flat brimmed sombrero from which dangled short tinsel tassels, a tight fitting *chaqueta* jacket with a glittering braid edging the lapels, and tight trousers tucked into shiny black boots.

When he saw I was a gringo, he nodded. "Señor. Do you have space for the señorita's carriage for the night?" He stiffened his shoulders, and with a hint of disdain continued. "We would have continued our journey for we only have a short distance to travel, but the señorita, she feels ill."

I toweled off my face and tugged my John B down on my head. "How many spans?"

"Three."

I gestured to the corral. "Over yonder. Six horses, six dollars to groom and grain. Three for the carriage."

He nodded sharply, a smile of satisfaction playing over his thin lips. "A fair price, señor. *Muchas gracias*." He paused. "I am a newcomer here. An inn, señor. Clean."

I nodded to a small inn across the narrow street. "Ask for Santo." I arched an eyebrow and with a wry chuckle added, "As clean as there is, amigo."

He grinned back. "*Gracias*."

That night, Salazar's courier failed to pick up the day's income, so I tucked it under my belt for safekeeping.

Salazar himself came by early next morning for his money. He grew excited when he spotted the carriage. I explained what had taken place. "What's the problem?" I asked.

He shook his head in excitement. "That is the carriage of the Señorita Damita Fidelia Cornia. Her father is the *alcalde* of all of Santa Fe, a most important and generous man. He who has the Don's favor is most generously rewarded."

I shrugged off Salazar's bubbling enthusiasm. I cared nothing of Corina, only Garrett.

Later that morning, the *caballero* from the day before and the driver came to the livery and hitched up the rig. They drove it across the street and stopped in front of Santo's.

Three scruffy cowpokes riding by reined up, looking on curiously.

The hair on the back of my neck bristled. The cowpokes were strangers. From the time I lived with the Kiowa, I learned to trust my feelings, and those I had about them jaspers were all bad. I eased forward, stopping at the corral just across the narrow street from the carriage, close enough to smell the sweat on the cowpokes' ponies.

Within minutes, a young woman wearing a veil and escorted by two other veiled women emerged from the inn and stepped into the carriage.

One of the cowboys whistled, and the other two laughed.

Before the driver could gee-haw the six-horse team, a skinny cowpoke with a patchy beard grabbed the leader's bridle. "Hold on there, amigo," he said, laughing. "Since we're strangers in town and ain't had time to get us no female company, how about introducing us to the señorita there?"

The *caballero* rode up. In a cold voice, he said, "The señorita is ill, señors. If you will excuse us, we must take her home."

A bearded cowpoke held up his hand. "Why, you bet. You go right along and get that little girl home."

The *caballero* nodded and reined around.

The bearded cowpoke shucked his sixgun and slammed the muzzle across the *caballero's* temple. The *caballero* dropped to the ground. His eyes icy, his voice cold, the cowboy aimed the sixgun at the driver. "Now, I said we want to meet the lady, you hear, Mexican?"

Dropping my hand to my side, I flipped the rawhide loop from the hammer of my Colt and stepped through the gate. I turned my back on the three, casually closing the gate.

One of them called out. "Where do you think you're going, cowboy?"

I turned back to them and grinned. From the corner of my eye, I could see the señorita staring at me from the window of her carriage. "Why, I was just figuring on helping you boys out of a bad situation."

The three frowned at each other. The one with the beard laughed. "What bad situation?"

"The one you're in right now."

The bearded gent shook his head. "You don't know what in the—"

Before he uttered another word, I shucked my Colt and blasted his sixgun from his hand.

Their horses reared and spun. Amid loud cursing and startled shouts, the one with the patchy beard tried to grab his sixgun, but my next slug clipped his reins, sending him tumbling over the cantle and sprawling on the cobblestone street.

They eventually managed to calm their frightened animals.

"All three of you could be staring up at waving grass right now, but the truth is I don't feel like killing anybody today." With the muzzle of my Colt, I gestured to the fallen *caballero*. "Now, all three of you. Pick up that boy and put him in the carriage."

Soberly, they did as I instructed.

When they closed the carriage door, I said, "You best not let me find out you been bothering these folks again. You understand?"

The younger cowboy gulped hard and nodded. The other two glared sullenly at me.

"Now git."

After the three disappeared around the corner, I approached the carriage. The young woman looked out at me. Like many young señoritas she was beautiful. She smiled gratefully. "*Gracias*, señor. We are in your debt."

I grinned. "Glad to help, miss. Too bad there's unmannerly yahoos like that around, but like I said, I'm glad I was here to give you a hand." I glanced up at the driver. "You need someone to ride along with you?"

He shook his head. "No, señor. *Gracias.*"

I winked at the señorita and stepped back. "Good luck."

After the carriage disappeared around a corner, I glanced after the three cowboys. I had a sneaky feeling I had not seen the last of those jaspers.

Chapter Seventeen

Maybe luck decided to latch on to my shirttail because I'd helped the Señorita Corina out of a bind, and maybe not. Whatever the reason, I drew into a winning hand the next night when I headed into the Cortez Barrio on the east side of the city.

After this barrio, there were only four remaining. More than once in the last three or four weeks, I worried that Garrett had moved on although I had asked no questions regarding him, and more than once I had also questioned my wisdom in not making a few discreet inquiries instead of playing my search so close to my vest.

From overheard conversations and idle talk, I learned the Cortez Barrio was one of the most treacherous neighborhoods in the city, not only for Mexicans, but especially for gringos. More than one fun-loving cowboy had been found on the street with his belly split open.

As I perused the cantinas that night, several malevolent looks were cast at me but no words were spoken, no threats made.

Near midnight, I pushed through the doors of a shabby cantina and paused just inside to survey the room. It was crowded, filled with loud curses and laughter almost overpowering the frenzied beat of the Spanish guitars.

After buying a whiskey, I found a table near one wall and plopped down, studying the room as unobtrusively as I could. I was beginning to think I'd missed Garrett again.

Suddenly, he strode through the door, worked his way through the crowd, and ducked under the bar. I lowered my head, peering from under my eyebrows. Garrett waved at someone against the far wall.

Moments later, three cowpokes elbowed up to the bar and nodded to Garrett. To my surprise, it was the three I'd braced for the señorita.

The four were engaged in a deep conversation. Suddenly, a chill ran through me when the young cowpoke with the patchy beard drew his finger down the side of his cheekbone, indicating the scar on my face.

Garrett stiffened. The smile on his face turned grim. He leaned forward and spoke rapidly, pointing to his own face.

The three cowboys nodded. Garrett grimaced and

shook his head, actions that made it obvious that he now knew I was in Santa Fe.

I had to move fast. Just as I started to rise, Garrett motioned for the three to lean forward. He spoke rapidly. They nodded and left. As soon as they disappeared out the front door, Garrett vanished through a door behind the bar.

Hurrying outside, I circled the block on foot, but before I reached the alley I heard hoofbeats fading into the night. I paused, staring into the darkness.

Just be patient, I told myself, trying to lay out my next step. More than one jasper had a scar on his face. Even if Garrett figured I was in Santa Fe, he could not know I had found his cantina. The smart thing for me to do was go about business as usual. In the meantime, I'd keep a close eye on his cantina and figure out his daily routine.

Then I would make my move.

Satisfied, I headed back to the livery.

Next morning, I answered a pounding on the door. I opened it to find a fresh-faced young lieutenant. Behind him sat four Union cavalrymen on their ponies. The lieutenant cleared his throat. "I'm looking for JC Thornton."

Behind the mounted soldiers, I spotted the three cowpokes I'd backed down. They sneered at me. I muttered a soft curse. *Garrett!* A chilling thought hit me. Maybe he had already left Santa Fe. Maybe he'd put the three owlhoots up to this so he'd have time to put miles between us. What other explanation?

I nodded. "What can I do for you, Lieutenant?"

His face grew hard. "You're coming with us, Thornton. The Army has no room for deserters."

The words hit me between the eyes like a singletree. I shot a look at the three cowpokes. Their sneers grew wider.

The lieutenant continued. "Are you going peaceable, Thornton, or do we have to take you?"

I drew a deep breath and tried to hang on to my temper. No sense in causing any further problems. That would just waste more time. And right now, time was as precious as gold. Holding up a hand, I replied in a calm voice. "No trouble, Lieutenant. No trouble."

With the lieutenant leading, I rode in an escort with two soldiers in front, two in back. A few miles outside of Santa Fe, we passed the gate to a large hacienda surrounded by smaller adobe and rock houses. Tendrils of smoke drifted from their chimneys.

From talk I'd heard in town, the estate belonged to Don Corina, the *alcalde* of Santa Fe, father of the young Senorita Corina.

With the young lieutenant standing stiffly at his side, Captain Steven Wingate looked up at me from behind his desk. Before him was an open folder. He wore a puzzled frown on his face. "To tell you the truth, Thornton, you're not listed here as a deserter."

He laid his hand on the folder. "This is a complete tally of federal deserters from eighteen-sixty-one to the end of April this year, seven years' worth, and there is no JC Thornton."

"That's because I was a Confederate, Captain. The Louisiana Three-Seventy-Seventh."

His eyes lit. "I was at Chattanooga. Brown's Ferry, in fact. We fought you boys." He grinned and shook his head. "Tell you the truth, those rebel yells still give me goosebumps."

I chuckled.

The lieutenant leaned over and whispered in the captain's ear. The older officer grew serious. "The lieutenant says he was informed that after leaving the Confederate Army, you joined the Union Army."

I shook my head. "Those jaspers told him wrong, Captain."

His forehead knit in puzzlement. "Why would they do that?"

Taking a deep breath, I said, "It's a long story, and it begins at Brown's Ferry."

For the next fifteen minutes, I related all that had taken place up until the present. I finished my story by saying, "I found Garrett in the cantina. Those three owlhoots work for him. I reckon he sent them to you figuring you'd hold me so I couldn't follow him." I shrugged. "That's it. The whole shebang."

The captain studied the folder on the desk for several

seconds, then looked up at the young officer at his side. "Lieutenant. Return Mr. Thornton's horse and gear." He rose from his desk and extended his hand. "I wish you good luck, Thornton."

Sitting in my saddle, I stared at the mountain peaks surrounding me, no doubt in my mind that Garrett had run. A grim smile tightened my lips. He had several hours on me, but first I had to find out just where he was headed. And I knew the three jaspers that could tell me.

The day was chilly. Back to the south, the rumble of thunder rolled across the pine-forested mountains. A few jagged lances of lightning danced through gray heavens. I snugged down in my bearskin coat and urged my pony into a trot. I wanted to reach town before the storm hit. Beneath tall pines on giant mountains in the middle of a lightning storm wasn't my idea of a pleasant day.

By the time I rode past the gate leading to the Corina hacienda, the churning clouds were overhead, dumping torrential rains and hurling down great trunks of chain lightning from which danced jagged forks of brilliant fire, cracking and splattering the forest.

Without warning, the grulla grunted and lunged sideways, stumbling over its front feet. That's when the sharp crack of the rifle reached my ears.

In the next instant, two more cracks split the frigid air, and a powerful blow caught me in the left shoulder, sending me tumbling from the back of my falling pony.

My head slammed into the rocky ground. Stars exploded, and the crash of lightning deafened me.

My instincts took over. I rolled, knowing I had to find cover the same way an animal knows. Somehow, I stumbled to my feet and lunged off the road, tumbling down a slope and bouncing off tree trunks. When I stopped rolling, I lay on my back, motionless, staring into the driving rain.

Voices drifted down from the road.

"Where'd he go?" I recognized the guttural voice of the bearded cowpoke.

"Down there somewhere," a voice replied.

Lightning crashed, lighting the forest with an eerie pale white glow.

I rolled onto my belly and squirmed behind a tree, grimacing against the numbing pain in my chest. I tried to move my left arm, but the excruciating pain almost knocked me out.

Despite the cold and the chilling rain, beads of sweat popped out on my face.

The bearded owlhoot asked, "You sure you got him?"

"You saw him fall off the horse, didn't you?"

"Go down there and see."

"Not me. I ain't going down there. You want to find him, you go yourself. I hit that jasper right in the heart, Fritz. He's down there staring at the sky and seeing nothing."

The rain grew heavier, and the lightning danced around us like it was a Saturday night stomp down at the Red Dog Saloon.

Fritz growled. "All right, boys. Let's get. I need something to warm my belly."

That was the last I remembered.

Chapter Eighteen

When I opened my eyes, a dusky young Mexican girl was smoothing the sheets stretched over me. Her eyes grew wide, and she hurried from the room.

Moments later, a beautiful young woman I recognized as Señorita Damita Fidelia Corina rushed into the room followed by her young *la criada*, handmaiden. She paused beside the bed and smiled warmly. "It is good to see you awake. You have been asleep for two days."

I tried to sit up, but a wave of dizziness washed over me.

She laid a slender hand against my shoulder and pressed me back. "No, señor. Do not move. You will disturb the wound." She spoke over her shoulder. "Serafina. Warm broth, pronto."

I dragged the tip of my tongue over my dry lips. "Obliged, ma' am."

She smiled at me as if I was a child. "I am the one in your debt, señor." Her dark eyes blazed. "Those gringos—" A frown of regret wrinkled her forehead.

I nodded slowly and forced a smile. "I understand, señorita."

Serafina hurried in with a large bowl of broth. It was thick and filling. After a few bites, I grew drowsy and drifted back into a fitful slumber, with thoughts of Hugh Garrett haunting my dreams.

The next time I saw the señorita, her father was at her side. He was effusive in his thanks for the help I had given her in Santa Fe.

Within another day, I was sitting up, demanding my clothes. Senorita Damita hurried in, followed by Serafina with her arms full of folded clothes. When I pointed out they were not mine, the senorita smiled coquettishly and replied that mine were dirty and torn, so she had taken it on herself to supply me with new ones as well as a razor for my beard.

To tell the truth, with the whiskers carved off my face, my hair scissored to a decent length, and outfitted with fresh duds, I felt like a new man. Still, while I was impatient to be on my way, I was as wobbly as a new-thrown foal. On the other hand, I did enjoy the company of the winsome and charming señorita.

The slug had entered inches below my collarbone

and exited behind my shoulder. After inspecting the wound a couple of days later the old Mexican doctor grunted, and with a wry grin muttered, "Well, señor, if you must have a hole in you, that is the best place."

I chuckled, and winced at the pain. It was hard to be funny with a hole in your shoulder.

Over the next few days, the señorita was a regular visitor, insisting I call her by her given name, Damita. She informed me that one of their laborers had found me after the storm. "We have your saddle and gear, but unfortunately, your horse was killed."

I bit my lip. The grulla and I had seen a heap of the southwest together. "He was a fine horse, dependable." I paused. "Maybe one day, I'll get another like him."

A sly smile slid over her face but I paid it no attention.

Once, while she was regaling me with stories of her family and their travails settling in New Mexico Territory, Don Corina and the young *caballero*, Platon Hernandez, entered, inquiring as to whether I knew who had bushwhacked me.

I nodded to Platon. "It was the three at the carriage."

His eyes grew hard. He dipped his head in deference to Don Corina. "I will find them for you, *Patron*."

Don Corina nodded briskly. "Do so."

By now, I was up and about. Despite Damita's attention and the unaccustomed luxury heaped on me, I grew restless to get back on Garrett's trail.

Within a week, my wound was scabbing over and I was

feeling right pert. That last day, Damita and I enjoyed a carriage ride around the estate. The grounds, the stock, the whole shebang was impressive even though toward the end of the tour my shoulder was beginning to throb.

Best I could figure out, the señorita had no suitors. The war and the influx of outsiders had driven many of the old, traditional families away, leaving only those that neither her aristocratic father nor she would approve.

The grandeur of baronial Spain was fast disappearing in New Mexico Territory, much as the charm and grace vanished in the devastated states of the antebellum South. While the Don was considered the *alcalde* of Santa Fe, the federal government had final jurisdiction. Looking out over the rolling valleys filled with grazing stock, I couldn't help feeling sorry for Don Corina and his family despite his wealth. His epoch in history was quickly disappearing.

Damita scooted around in the carriage seat to face me. "You wish to leave?"

I grinned. "Is it that obvious?"

A sad smile played over her lips. "My father thinks very highly of you."

"And I of him. He's a good man."

"You are always welcome here."

I read between the lines, and for a moment wondered if I was playing the fool by following my hard-headed determination to get the truth from Garrett. After all, what would it accomplish? Even if court-martial records were corrected, no one would change his mind. What was done, was done. Accusations, once hurled, though disproven, forever remain.

But then I knew what it would achieve. It would give me back a good name, even if I was the only one to know. When a jasper goes to his grave, that's all that really counts. "Thank you," I whispered, laying my hand on hers. I wanted to say more, but I couldn't find the words.

She smiled sadly, then spoke rapidly to the driver.

A few minutes later, we pulled up to the corral by the barn. Half a dozen magnificent horses lifted their heads and stared at us.

"These are my father's prize stallions."

I whistled softly, taking in the almost perfect conformation of the animals. "Fine horseflesh. Mighty fine."

She gestured to one. "That copper-colored one. He is Pedro, which means rock. He is my father's favorite. Never has the animal failed my father."

"Like I said, mighty fine. Magnificent. I don't reckon I've ever seen a better animal."

Damita smiled up at me. "He is yours."

That night in his gathering room after the senorita had retired to her bedroom, Don Corina poured another glass of peach brandy and handed it to me as we stood in front of the fireplace, enjoying the soaking warmth of the leaping flames.

"To your safe journey," he said, toasting me.

I accepted the toast and nodded slowly. "But your gift of the stallion is too generous."

He arched an eyebrow. "You do not care for Pedro?"

"No." I shook my head emphatically. "He is a fine animal, but much too valuable for me to accept as a gift."

"He is yours, Señor Thornton."

"But—"

The Don insisted, reminding me that I had saved his only daughter and heir from a fate meted out only by the demons of hell.

The more I protested, the more resolute he became. Finally, he held up his hand to stay our disagreement, then gestured to a richly upholstered chair in front of the fireplace. "Sit. Let me speak."

After the Don sat, he hesitated a moment, staring into the crystal glass cupped in both hands. His brows were knit with concentration as he struggled to find the right words. "My family has lived here for over two hundred years, Señor Thornton, since Philip the Fourth of Spain gave my great-great-grandfather a land grant for all of what is now New Mexico Territory." With a wry bitterness in his tone, he continued. "As you can see, there have been many changes in the lives of me and my people, of my *sirvientes*, monumental changes that cause me great concern over the welfare of my daughter." He paused. "Please forgive me if I sound, how should I say . . . if I sound portentous, but for generations my family has enjoyed and maintained an aristocratic life. Now, after the great war back in the East, I know this is no longer possible, not with the westward drive of the United States in its quest for eminent domain, not with the Union Armies taking control of the territory."

He paused to drink deeply of his brandy. With a sad smile, he continued. "My generation will be the last of the old ways. There are none to whom I would trust my Damita." He stared deep into my eyes. "But, I would trust her with you."

If I'd had a mouthful of brandy I would have choked. I thought to laugh, but I knew that would offend the Don, which I would never do. "I appreciate the confidence, Don Corina, but—"

He held his hand to stop me. "Let me speak, señor, *por favor*. I have considered these words many days. From your actions, you are an honorable man, a noble man. The one for whom you work speaks of you admirably. In the conversations you and I have had over the last few days, I have discerned you are an educated man." He paused, nodded firmly. "I know of your search from what I have learned from my people at the soldiers' fort. All I will say is that once you have settled your mind about what you must do, as an old man and doting father, I would be pleased to see you return. My estate is vast and with a firm hand, will be productive for many generations to come despite the invasion of outsiders."

I was speechless, a state most uncommon to me. Quickly, I sorted through the thoughts tumbling about in my head. There was no arguing with the man. His mind was made up. That was obvious. Besides, Señorita

Damita Fidelia was the most beautiful, the most charming, and the most gracious lady that a scruffy jasper like me could ever hope to meet, much less wed.

The trouble was, I had no feeling for her, not the marrying kind.

The old Don must have read my mind, for he grunted and said, "I know you have had little time to know each other, but I think you are friends, and there is nothing which is a more sound foundation for love than friendship."

I couldn't argue with the wise old man on that. Not one whit. I'd be lying if I said I knew exactly what I was going to do. I drew a deep breath. "Look, Don Corina. I've got a job to do." I glanced around the rich furnishings of the great room. "You're good people. Señorita Damita"—I shrugged—"she's a wonderful woman. I do like her but I must finish what I've got to do. And when it is all over, you have my promise I will return."

His craggy face lit in a bright grin until I added, "Then we can discuss of what you speak. Who knows, perhaps by then, Señorita Damita will have pledged herself to one of her own."

He arched an eyebrow and held up the remainder of his brandy. "Until then, Señor Thornton. Until then."

As I climbed the stairs bearing a candle to light the way to my room, I thought of Lucy Coulter back on the Llano, and a strange sense of guilt washed over me.

Chapter Nineteen

That night, Don Corina, accompanied by Platon, the young *caballero,* awakened me. Platon was haggard and drawn. The Don informed me that neither Garrett nor the three owlhoots were in Santa Fe. No one knew where they went.

Some said they had ridden to Kansas to join a renegade band of northern and southern deserters intent on looting and burning settlements all over the Midwest.

Others claimed they headed to California, and still others, to Wyoming.

After the Don left, I lay staring into the darkness above my head.

By now, summer was drawing near. For the last year, I had tracked Garrett. And I would continue, but the leads

I had now were too flimsy. Garrett could be anywhere from Indian Territory to the Pacific Ocean.

So now what, JC? Hang around here or ride back to Texas?

Whatever drive, whatever craving a jasper's emotions and dreams have on him, I've never been able to understand. I don't reckon I ever will, for the remainder of the night I dredged up a dozen reasons to stay at the hacienda. On the other hand, I came with another dozen as to why I should ride back to Texas.

With mixed feelings, I rode out the next morning for Texas. For the next three or four days, I constantly questioned the wisdom of my decision, telling myself that the smart move would be to turn around and go back.

Who knows, maybe the Don was right. A friendship is essential to lasting love. I didn't know if that little bit of philosophy was true or not, but then I wasn't the brightest candle on the tree either.

I could build a life in the beautiful mountains surrounding Santa Fe. If Garrett was to surface, sooner or later I would hear of him. In the meantime, I would be doing something worthwhile with my life instead of tracking across endless spaces searching for a will-o'-the-wisp.

Still, there were the Coulters. Deep down, I knew that I had to return. Instinct told me that only by being with them could I get them out of my mind.

I finally reconciled my decision with the guess that

Garrett headed to Kansas. Raiders and looters were his style. And if they were active on the Great Plains, we'd hear about them down in Kimble County.

My first hint of serious trouble came in the middle of a heat wave when I hit Palo Duro Canyon a week later. I had dropped off the Staked Plains down into the canyon, deliberately staying in the shade close to the yellow and lavender canyon walls, some of which stretched eight hundred feet above my head.

In the distance, perpendicular parapets of red mudstone streaked with scars of white gypsum added to the spectacular vista of a colorful canyon dotted with green patches of scrubby cedar.

The Kiowa in me made me spookier than a grasshopper in a yard full of hungry chickens. When riding through unfamiliar country, I always built a small fire during the day for coffee and warm broth or broiled venison, and then moved on to a cold camp for the night.

Instead of camping near a pool of water in the middle of the canyon, I reined Pedro back into a thick growth of cedar in the mouth of a narrow canyon leading off the main branch. I was looking forward to a cup of thick, black coffee and a few strips of fried bacon wrapped in johnnycakes.

I loosened the cinch and went about gathering dry wood. Just as I squatted to lay the fire, Pedro snorted. His ears pricked forward. Instantly, the hair on the back of my neck bristled. I glanced around. Through the cedar, I saw a band of Comanche riding southeast. They paused at the tiny pool of water in the middle of the canyon floor. Only about a quarter of a mile distant, they were close enough to spot the war paint on their animals. "Easy, boy, easy," I whispered, laying branches on the ground and rising to pinch his nostrils.

For the next hour, we watched the band slowly disappear in the distance. Now I was in a quandary. Continue on down the canyon and risk running into them, or remain behind, forced to tag along after the band.

Not eager to leave the canyon, I glanced at the rim. There, above me, was that part of Texas known as the Llano Escadado, or the Staked Plains, so called by early Spanish explorers because the plains were so flat and treeless that early travelers drove stakes every so often so they could find their way back to their camp each night.

On the Staked Plains, a jasper can spot any moving object within five miles and a fire at night at ten miles.

I scratched Pedro's nose and muttered. "Reckon our smart move is just to hang back. Give them a day, and then we'll move out."

Pedro nickered and jerked his head. I frowned as he looked back into the narrow canyon behind us and nickered again. His nostrils flared, and he tugged against my grip on the bridle.

"Something back there, boy?"

Holding his bridle, I led the big animal through the thick growth of cedar into the canyon. Fifty or so yards back, we came upon a small pool of fresh water, fed by water dripping from a tiny fissure in the sandstone.

From the sign, the pool was frequented by the canyon's animals. Tracks of mule deer, coyote and rabbit were mixed with wild turkey tracks. Pedro and I, side by side, drank our fill and then I topped off my canteen.

Farther back in the canyon were patches of sideoats gramma and big bluestem grass.

Farther back, the canyon was so narrow that only when the sun was directly overhead did it light the floor below. We spent the afternoon in cool shadows. Pedro grazed, and I sprawled on the ground staring at the canyon walls absently.

I frowned at what appeared to be a ledge between two columns of yellow and gray limestone. Suddenly, I realized I was staring at what looked like part of a trail to the rim. Curious, I ambled over to the canyon wall and behind a thick cedar and discovered a narrow trail that led upward.

About three feet wide, the trail ascended through wide fissures, then at times along the outer walls of the canyon before disappearing back into what looked to be natural tunnels.

Ten minutes later, I topped out on the canyon rim.

Far to the southeast, I spotted smoke. I guessed it was the band that had passed earlier. The sun was quickly dropping toward the horizon. I turned to head back down and froze.

Below, a mile or so to the west rode another band of

Indians, coming in my direction. I dropped to my belly and peered over the rim, hoping their keen eyes had not picked up my silhouette.

They continued their leisurely journey until they pulled up and starting setting up camp just a few hundred yards from the mouth of the canyon.

Pulse racing, I hurried back down and moved my plunder deeper into the canyon.

After hobbling Pedro, I eased to the edge of the cedar where I could keep an eye on the camp. By now the sun had set and the darkness prevented any identification of the tribe.

I slept in bits and pieces during the night. Well before sunrise, the Indians had their fires going. As the fingers of false dawn pushed away the darkness, I spotted a figure riding in my direction, his pony loaded with canteens.

I muttered a soft curse. Apparently, the water hole around which they had camped had been worked dry. Obviously, they were aware of the water back in the canyon. Quickly, I hurried back to the pool and hastily erased our sign before slipping deeper into the canyon. I found a spot under a thick cedar where I could watch the tiny pool of sweet water.

From the paint on the warrior I saw he was of the Yamparika Comanche. Red and white dots covering his face indicated he was a young warrior searching for his first coup. The unaltered feather in his head indicated this was his first war journey.

I held my breath as he knelt and filled the canteens. Time dragged. Finally, he finished. I breathed easier as he looped the canteens over the saddle horn of his pony.

Suddenly, he froze, staring at the ground.

A cold chill ran up my spine. What had he spotted?

Glancing around suspiciously, the young warrior knelt and ran his finger over the ground. He rose, looked in my direction, then turned back to his pony.

I breathed a sigh of relief.

Without warning, he turned back, this time easing in my direction, his eyes studying the ground at his feet.

Silently, I slipped my knife from its scabbard.

He drew closer.

Finally, he was just beyond the cedar behind which I crouched, close enough that I could smell the bear grease he wore against insects.

The feathery sound of his moccasins told me he was circling the cedar. I circled in the other direction, quickly sheathing my knife and shucking my sixgun as I came up behind him.

Without warning, he spun, his teeth bared.

I aimed for his temple, but faster than a striking rattler, the young warrior jerked his head aside and grabbed his knife. With a guttural cry, he lunged at me, slashing the wicked blade back and forth.

Leaping aside, I swept the muzzle backhanded, the front sight catching his forehead and ripping the skin, pouring blood into his eyes and down across his dotted face.

He staggered back, caught himself, then lurched forward, at the same time hooking the blade of his knife up. I threw myself backwards, but the tip of his blade bounced off the buckle of my gun belt and sliced open the front of my linen shirt. Using the Colt again, I slammed his arm aside and threw a left hook into his jaw.

The game young warrior tried unsuccessfully to catch himself from falling, but he went sprawling to the ground. In the same motion, he rolled to his feet, but I met him with another left, this one straight to the point of his jaw.

He collapsed like a wet rag.

Moving quickly, I led Pedro onto the trail leading to the rim before returning to remove sign from the hidden entrance. Knowing the Comanches' skill at reading sign and track, I had no doubt they would eventually find the trail, but I hoped to buy enough time to put a few miles between us.

Chapter Twenty

I rode due east against my better judgment for that would take me straight into Indian Territory, but I had no choice for now—at least two bands of Comanche were behind me.

Pedro gave me everything I asked for. We left the canyon in a gallop for a couple of miles then dropped into a controlled three-beat canter that ate up the flat prairie.

Mid-afternoon, I took a chance and cut southeast, hoping to somehow avoid the Comanche raiding parties behind and any bands of Indians roaming out of the territory to my left.

For the next week, I rode through a tableland of rolling hills covered with thin grama and mesquite. The growth was so thick that a jasper couldn't see a hundred yards. More than once, spooked wild longhorns and buffalo tore through the scrub, sending my hand flashing to my sixgun and my heart into my throat.

The grass grew thinner as I continued southeast. I figured it to be sometime in June when I crossed what I thought was the Concho River, a shallow, slow-running body with sandy shores baked hot by the sun and populated with dozens of sunning rattlesnakes.

A week later, I thought I had died and gone to heaven when I spotted the first of the Central Texas hill country where rocky canyons, rolling hills, and spreading liveoaks enjoyed the musical gurgling and freshness of cool streams twisting their way to the Colorado.

Soon I began spotting familiar landmarks, and late one evening, I hit the Llano River at a spot not more than two or three miles west of the Coulter spread.

The waning moon wouldn't rise for another three hours, but the starlight illuminated the countryside sufficiently for me to ride on in. I had butterflies in my stomach thinking about seeing the Coulters again, Lucy really.

And then I felt a tinge of guilt about Damita.

From time to time in my journey from Santa Fe, I had thought of the two, but the trip was so dangerous that the luxury of daydreaming about two beautiful and charming women was an indulgence that could separate an hombre from his hair right fast.

* * *

I guessed it was around ten o'clock when I reined up Pedro at the edge of the forest and peered at the darkened cabin. I could smell the wood smoke from the dying embers in the fireplace.

Before I could urge my pony forward, the frenzied barking of a dog broke the silence of the night.

The cabin remained dark but moments later came a woman's voice. "Who's out there?"

It was Lucy. I wondered why she called out instead of Floyd. I shrugged. Maybe he was on a cattle selling or buying trip. "It's me, Mrs. Coulter. JC Thornton."

Instantly the dim glow of lantern light shone through the windows of the cabin. The door opened a crack. "Come in, Mr. Thornton."

The dog continued yapping. Little Ben cried out. "Hush up, Abraham."

Two dark figures emerged from the barn.

By the time I reached the cabin, Nat Gallatin and Wishbone were waiting.

Wishbone grunted. "Well?"

I knew what he meant. "Not this time."

"Snuck away again, huh?"

"Slicker than calf slobber."

Lucy Coulter had lost weight. She had dark circles under her eyes, but she still had her ready smile and bright disposition, at least until she informed me that her husband was dead.

Stunned by the news, I looked at Wishbone. He

nodded. "Comanche. Best we could figure from the sign, they jumped him on the way back from the fort where he'd gone to pick up supplies and the weekly mail."

Later, as Nat, Wishbone, and I headed to the barn with the brindle mongrel Abraham trailing behind sniffing at me, the bow-legged cowpoke explained. "Rust pulled out. Cattle drive came through back west a month or so ago. He hooked on to it."

"What about Wingo?"

With pained resignation, Nat gestured to the bunkroom by the barn. "He's in there, snoring away."

"Yep," Wishbone growled. "He was planning to ride out when Mr. Coulter got hisself kilt dead." His voice dropped lower. "I figure he's done set his cap for Miz Coulter, seeing as how she's now a widow with property. He tried to take over running the place, but Miz Coulter wouldn't have none of it."

I shook my head. "So, she's figuring on staying on?"

"Reckon so. According to what she told us after the burying, she ain't got no place to go. She reckons on building the place up just like her husband."

Nat chuckled. "Miz Coulter, she's a mighty determined lady. I figure she can do just about whatever she sets her mind to."

Those were my thoughts exactly.

The next weeks passed without incident, long hot days of back-breaking labor, tending stock, building fences, looking after the thousand and one small jobs that are essential to a successful ranch.

Little Ben was fast becoming an accomplished horseman astride the Indian mustang I had given him. Callie stayed right on her mama's heels, and from what I saw, provided a great deal of help for Mrs. Coulter.

Wingo remained his old truculent self, blown up with self-importance, and I quickly noticed what Wishbone meant when he said Mrs. Coulter kept Wingo on a short lease. The burly jasper constantly offered opinions and suggestions about running the spread and when Lucy Coulter refused to listen to him, he would complain to us, "That woman's going to run this place into the ground, mark my words."

Wishbone and Nat just grinned.

And of course, Wingo wasn't any too pleased to see my ugly face. And of course, I just paid him no mind. And of course, it just aggravated him that much more.

From time to time, I ran across Indian sign. Once when little Ben and I were bringing the cows into the corral for the night, I noticed the tracks of three Indian ponies at the edge of the forest.

I passed word on to Wishbone and Nat to be doubly wary.

One day after I'd been back a month or so, Ben rode up to tell me Mrs. Coulter would like to see me if it were convenient.

I paused in the open doorway of the cabin. Lucy Coulter had her back to me when I cleared my throat. Dishtowel in hand, she spun, and a bright smile played over her face. "Mr. Thornton. Please, come in." She gestured to the table. "I made some sweet dough cakes and coffee." She hesitated when she saw the frown come on my face. "I need to talk, and you're the only one I trust," she added matter-of-factly.

Curious as to the subject of her conversation, I sat at the heavy sawbuck table as she poured two cups of coffee and slid a platter heaped with sweet dough cakes between us. After she sat, she fixed her green eyes on mine and bluntly asked, "Do you plan on staying or riding on?"

I hesitated, surprised at such a direct question.

She hastened to add, "The reason I ask is that I don't want to waste your time if you are planning on riding out."

Nodding slowly, I sorted my thoughts. "Like I told you when I came back, Mrs. Coulter, I—"

She interrupted. "Please, JC, call me Lucy. We've known each almost a year." A comely smile parted her lips. "I don't think we have to be so formal, do you?"

I grinned. "No. No, we don't . . . Lucy."

"Fine. So, what are your plans?"

"Like I told you when I rode in, I didn't find Hugh Garrett. When I came back, I was planning on staying. Still am. Same as last time. No pay, just a place to throw my soogan and some beans and bacon." I paused and then added, "Until I hear something about Garrett again."

Her face beamed. "Good. I can handle that. Like I said earlier, I trust you, JC. I need someone I can seek advice from about the ranch. I couldn't go to the others, because . . . well"—she struggled for the right words— "because the truth is, Nat is too young. Wishbone—good hand, but that's all, a good hand. He knows his cows. Beyond that"—she shrugged—"then there's Wingo. He fancies running the ranch. He's been my biggest problem. When I suggest we break more land for pasture, he disagrees. I want more fences, he says we don't need them." She paused, shivered, then confessed, "I've never cared for the man. I tried to talk Floyd out of hiring him, but we needed the help."

"Why don't you just fire him?"

She sipped her coffee and broke off a bite-sized chunk of dough cake. "Because he has a gun, and there are Indians about."

I looked at her in surprise.

She laughed. "I'm not blind. I've seen tracks along the river's edge and between here and the fort."

With a wry grin, I agreed. "They are about."

With a teasing smile, she asked, "What were you going to do, keep me in the dark about them, JC?"

I arched an eyebrow. "Just couldn't see no sense in worrying you for nothing."

She laughed, and for the next thirty minutes, I learned her life story, from West Virginia to Kimble County, Texas. "And so when the war took everything from me, I accepted Floyd's offer of marriage and we came out here." Her bottom lip quivered slightly, and a tear glistened in eyes. "He's dead, and again, I'm alone, but now I have something to work for, this land, sixty-four-hundred acres." She set her jaw and her eyes grew determined. "I plan to build something for Ben and Callie, one way or another."

At that moment, I truly admired that woman, all grit and determination. A true western woman to stand beside her man and help him carve a niche for themselves out of the wilderness.

"Well, Mrs., I mean, Lucy. As long as you got Wishbone and me, you won't be alone."

A look of gratitude filled her eyes. "I hoped that's what you would say, JC I truly did."

I nodded. "Don't worry about Wingo. I'll take care of him."

She smiled gratefully.

Chapter Twenty-one

Before I left the cabin I made up my mind that at the first opportunity I'd set Wingo straight about his place on the ranch, and if it didn't come up then I would force it. Lucy was the boss. We didn't question her decisions unless she asked our opinion.

I figured even Wingo with his pea-sized brain could grasp those two givens.

Life has a way of working problems out, and I'd no sooner returned to the pole fence I had been building than Wingo came trotting across the prairie toward me.

He leaped off his horse and stomped up behind me while I was bent over, pulling on my leather work gloves. "What was you and Miz Coulter talking about, Thornton?"

I looked around into those beady black eyes that

161

reminded me of a June bug. I snugged the last glove down around my fingers. "I don't reckon that's any of your business, Wingo."

His eyes blazed. He stepped forward, his body only inches from mine, and jabbed a sausage like finger in my chest. "I'm running things around here what with Coulter gone. So I say it is my business."

I studied him for a moment, and then a faint grin played over my lips.

He frowned, confused at the smile on my face.

"In fact," I said, "I'm glad you rode over. Saves me having to run you down."

His frown deepened.

Before he could respond, I announced flatly, "You're fired. Get your plunder and get out before dark."

He gaped at me in disbelief, his black eyes bulging. "Why–why—" His eyes narrowed in anger and the muscles in his jaws writhed like a nest of snakes. "You can't do that. I'm—"

"You're fired. That's what you are. Now, either you get your gear or I'll get it for you."

He glared murderously at me. His rugged face grew red. I could see the fury building in him like a steam engine, ready to explode.

With a guttural scream that must have echoed for miles, he drew his big fist back.

Before he could throw his punch, I kicked him in the kneecap, and when he doubled over, I slammed a left hook into his bearded jaw, snapping his head around.

He tried to recover, but I followed up with a right up-percut, smashing his nose over his face and sending him stumbling backward.

It's true. Hindsight is always perfect. I should have stayed on him like fleas on a hound dog, but I hesitated just long enough for the big man to lumber to his feet and smash a ham-sized fist into my jaw, sending me tumbling over the fence.

When I looked up, he was holding a small log over his head like a club. A guttural growl came through his bared teeth as he slammed the log down. I rolled aside just in time, then kicked my heel backward, catching him behind his knee and sending him to the ground.

I leaped to my feet and waded into that big hombre.

Wingo had me by fifty pounds, and he was solid, as solid as the hardpan in front of the cabin. Keeping my head down and jaw protected, I waded into him, pound-ing my fists into his rock-hard belly, driving him back-ward while he rained heavy blows on my shoulders.

Suddenly, he grabbed my shoulders and threw me aside. He hesitated, drawing his shoulders back and glaring at me. "Arggh! I'm going to break you in half, Thornton. Then we'll see who the big stud is around here. I—"

I threw a sizzling right that stopped him in his tracks. Before he could spit out the two teeth I'd loosened, I slammed three more devastating blows into his jaw.

He staggered backward, shaking his massive head. He blinked his eyes, snorted like a charging bull, and lunged at me. I had seen the same move a hundred, no, a thousand times growing up with the Kiowa. I stepped back, grabbed his thick arm with one hand, his vest with the other, fell to the ground on my back, and flipped him head over heels.

He crashed to the ground, stunned.

Before he could move, I was straddling his chest, the tip of my knife pressed into the flesh under his chin. "One wrong move, Wingo, and I'll put this blade in that pig brain of yours, understand?"

The fear in his eyes told me he understood.

"Good. You gather your plunder and ride out. I see you around here again, I'll kill you. That's not a promise. That's a fact."

Within the hour, Wingo had disappeared in the direction of the fort. Wishbone squatted by my side as I knelt at the river's edge and washed the blood from my face. "He ain't going to forget this, you know that don't you, JC?"

Gingerly, I touched the swelling on my cheekbone. I chuckled. "I don't reckon I will either."

The Coulter spread ran over two miles along the river's shore and about five deep. If heaven's a ranch, it couldn't offer much more than this spread with its lush valleys, deep canyons, and a dozen sweet water springs feeding the river.

Once when Coulter and I were riding back from the

fort, he'd made a sweeping gesture with his hand and proudly announced that this was what he had looked for all his life. "Everything a man could want."

He was right. It was everything a man could want. I couldn't help wondering how many generations had viewed this very country and uttered the same words. My Kiowa father, Big Horse, had spoken often of various tribes that had populated the country from the time of the great flood.

They were many and varied, most with the dream of living a good life with their God and their family.

Now, the white man was beginning to possess the country, to push the red man aside as the Indian had pushed those before him aside. Sometimes I reminded myself with a touch of wry humor that the white man would be the next to be displaced. By whom, I had no idea, but I guessed within a few hundred years it would happen.

As on all spreads, even the children had their chores.

Little Ben was the wood gatherer for the main house, and to make his job easier and more productive, I showed him how to build a travois on which to carry dry wood, but with the caution that he never pick up branches or small logs without first checking their shade for sleeping rattlesnakes.

I had ridden back west one morning to check on drifting stock when I spotted Ben near the mouth of a narrow box canyon dutifully stacking branches and small logs on the travois. I looked around but Abraham was nowhere in sight.

To my alarm, I saw that instead of using a limb or pole to disturb the branches lying on the carpet of leaves, Ben was using the toe of his brogan.

I reined toward him and urged Pedro into a trot. Ben kicked a small log, then looked around when he heard me approaching. A broad grin leaped to his face and he waved.

Suddenly, a dark, rope-like figure exploded from behind the log. Instinct took over as the Colt leaped into my hand and I fired.

The slug caught the rattler in mid-strike, exploding his head.

Ben just stood wide-eyed, stunned. He stared at the thick–bodied snake writhing in its death throes at his feet. The boy's face grew pale. His lips quivered, and tears filled his eyes.

I dismounted quickly. I didn't think he'd been hit, but I checked him over just to be sure. He was fine, and then I got angry. By the time I finished skinning the boy alive, the tears were running down his cheeks.

Suddenly, Abraham came crashing through the underbrush. When he spotted the writhing snake, he grabbed it and shook it ferociously. Abruptly, he yapped and jumped sideways, dropping the snake.

With a growl, he started biting at his shoulder.

Ben's tears dried. He reached down to the dog. "What's the matter, boy? Huh?"

Abraham wheeled and snapped at the boy, then raced into the forest, disappearing among the liveoak and berry briars.

"What happened?" On the verge of tears again, Ben looked up at me. "What's wrong with Abraham?"

I had an idea but I didn't voice it to little Ben. I figured when the dog shook the rattler, one of the fangs still filled with venom struck him in the shoulder. A bizarre twist of luck, but I had seen stranger doses of misfortune. "Beats me, boy," I lied. "I wouldn't worry about it. He'll probably be waiting for you back at the cabin." And then I raked him over the coals once again for being so careless.

"I didn't mean to be so hard on the boy, Lucy, but he came within inches of taking a heavy dose of venom. It was a big rattler, and I figure he had a heap of poison built up in him."

She smiled gratefully and laid her hand on my arm. "I'm just glad you were there, JC." Her smile faded. "You really think that's what happened to Abraham? Ben loves that mangy dog."

"Could be. He was shaking that rattler something fierce."

Ben didn't take supper with us that night—too embarrassed according to his mother. But by the next night, like all youngsters, what happened the day before was forgotten as if it had never happened, though off and on throughout the day he did call for Abraham.

Lucy fried up a pan of cornbread and a batch of fish Ben had brought in from the traps we had built. Around mouthfuls of grub, the boy looked up at me and said, "You sure are fast with that sixgun, Mr. Thornton. I ain't never seen nobody that fast. How'd you learn? Can you teach me?"

His mother hushed him but I just grinned. "An old man taught me, Ben. Professor R Wellington Thornton of the Thornton's Traveling Circus."

Ben frowned. "He your pa?"

"No. I took his name because I didn't have a white man's name. He found me with the Kiowa when I was twelve. He talked my Kiowa pa, Big Horse, into letting me go with him and learn the ways of the white man. Big Horse agreed. He knew the days of the Indian were numbered, and I would be better off knowing the ways of my own people. He was a wise man."

"But he was an Indian. How could he be a wise man?"

Lucy's face turned crimson. "That's enough, young man. You know better than to be rude."

Ben looked up at her puzzled, having no idea what he had done.

I grew serious. "Listen to me, Ben. Remember what I say. Wisdom has nothing to do with a man's race or color. I've known white men dumber than skunks— Indians too, and I've also known a heap of Indians that could give smart lessons to some white people."

Chagrinned and embarrassed, the boy ducked his head and muttered, "I'm sorry."

I laid my hand on his shoulder. "Forget it. Anyway, I became part of the professor's show, putting on shooting exhibitions."

His eyes bright with excitement, Ben exclaimed, "Can he teach me like he taught you?"

For several moments, I studied the youngster, then slowly shook my head. "He died when I was about seventeen. Just got sick one day and was gone the next." That was a lie, but I saw no reason to tell the boy. The professor had been murdered, and his killer tried to plant me, but I beat him to the draw.

Ben's brow puckered as he carefully pondered my words, then a smile replaced the frown. "You can teach me. Will you, huh? Will you?"

I winked at Lucy. "We'll see, boy. We'll see."

Chapter Twenty-two

Abraham never returned. From time to time, I'd spot Ben looking out over the fields and forest for the dog. I felt bad keeping the truth from him until one day he stopped me and said, "I don't think Abraham is coming back."

I arched an eyebrow. "Oh? Why's that?"

His forehead wrinkled in concentration. "I been thinking about it. I bet when he shook that snake, he got struck. He probably died from the poison."

Studying him closely, I saw no tears in his eyes, but a matter-of-fact acceptance of Nature's hard truths. I laid my hand on his small shoulder. "Could be," I replied. "Could be."

*   *   *

Over the next few months, several drifters stopped to take meals and sleep over, but none of them provided any leads on Hugh Garrett, nor did any of my weekly visits to the Kimble Emporium, the local saloon at the fort.

From time to time, we'd run across Indian sign, but most of the trouble of which we heard was farther south and east. That puzzled me. It was as if the war parties were deliberately circling around us, but why?

I got my answer, or at least a partial answer, in the middle of July when a patrol from Fort Kimble stopped in to water their animals. The young lieutenant relayed information gained from Indian scouts working for the cavalry that the war parties wanted to stay as far away from the forts as possible.

According to messages sent from one fort to the other, any depredations were occurring at least a full day's ride from the garrisons.

"Reckon I ain't complaining about that," muttered Nat that night as we lay on our soogans. "It's a good feeling knowing them redsticks is staying away from us."

I chuckled. "Don't go getting too confident, Nat. That's the time they hit, the time you least expect them."

Two days later when torrential rains hit the hill country, I wasn't surprised. I had been expecting a drastic change in the weather. A few days earlier, we had a strong south wind that gradually shifted to the east and then northeast.

Clouds scudded overhead, and the tingling smell of ozone filled the air. I reckoned it was what was left of one of those hurricanes that had plowed into the coast and rolled northward. What few experiences I'd had with those big storms, I knew they could last for hours, even days. And that's when cattle started getting spooky.

That first morning, the rain gusted in patches. The gray clouds rolled and tumbled across the heavens. Leaving Nat with Lucy and the children, Wishbone and I drove the stock to a box canyon a mile or so from the cabin. The canyon was an ideal holding pen for the cows and mules for we had previously constructed a rail fence across its mouth.

A mile east was another box canyon, that one with a hidden trail leading to the rim above.

Just before sunset that first day of rain, a young private pulled up from the fort to inform us a company was pulling out and heading east to pursue renegade Comanche and Kiowa who were raiding settlements from Austin to San Antonio.

"We're leaving two platoons at the fort," he said. "There've been no reports of renegades in our area but keep a sharp watch anyhow."

For two more days it rained and the wind blew, at times to gale force. The river began to rise, slowly creeping up the hill toward the cabin. Great trees, uprooted by the strong winds, floated downriver.

The morning of the third day dawned bright and clear, and with it came a band of screaming Indians, Comanche I guessed at first.

Both the rock cabin and the bunkhouse were veritable forts, and because of the rain, too sodden to fire. Wishbone and Nat were in the bunkhouse. I'd been in the cabin drinking coffee when the war party struck.

Suddenly, there was the crack of a rifle, and a scream just outside the door, which burst open and Nat staggered inside, blood pumping from his shoulder. "Indians!" he shouted. "Hundreds of them!"

I leaped to my feet and slammed the door while Lucy hurried to Nat's side. "Close the shutters and grab a gun," I yelled to Ben while peering through a gun port and clacking a cartridge into the Henry Yellowboy. I hesitated, spotting several Kiowa with the Comanche. I cursed, and in the back of my mind I wondered about Red Eagle, my brother. Just as quickly I dismissed the thought. He was a man of peace and tolerance, not renegades like these.

While a dozen or so warriors raced around the cabin firing their carbines at the wooden shutters, another dozen swarmed into the corral. I clenched my teeth, hoping Wishbone had spotted them in time to slip away.

Slugs and three-foot long arrows thumped into the heavy shutters.

The Comanche and Kiowa were skilled warriors, offering small targets utilizing the technique of digging a heel into their horses' rumps, which let them cling to the offside of their ponies and shoot under the animals' necks.

I touched off a shot.

Behind me, Nat struggled to his feet despite Lucy's protests. "I can shoot," he growled, staggering to a rear window and rapidly emptying his sixgun at the yapping warriors racing around the cabin.

"Take your time," I called out, touching off another shot. "I got a feeling we're in here for the long haul."

I glanced to my right. Carbine tucked into her shoulder, Lucy fired out the gun port. Soon the cabin was filled with the acrid stench of gunsmoke stinging our nostrils.

Nat growled. "Can't see them heathens. They's hiding behind their ponies."

The only part of the warrior visible when he rode in attack mode was the shin of his leg cast over the rump of the horse. "Shoot for the leg."

He snorted. "I ain't that good a shot."

"Then shoot the horse."

I touched off another shot, this time catching a warrior's shin, knocking him from his galloping pony. He hit the ground and rolled to his feet, but I put another slug into his chest, knocking him backward.

Nat fired, and a horse went down. With the grace and agility of a wildcat, the Comanche warrior threw himself from the falling pony and landed on his moccasined feet in a mad dash for the forest.

Another rifle cracked, and the brave lunged forward into the mud.

Without warning, the warriors vanished back into the surrounding forest. The day grew silent.

Ben yipped, "We whipped them, we whipped them!"

Lucy and I looked at each other with a wry grin. "Don't count on it, boy," I said. "At least, not right yet."

Lucy went to sit on the bed beside Callie who had not uttered a word throughout the fight.

Nat leaned up against the wall, sweat pouring down his pale face. He forced a faint grin. "At least, we run 'em off this time, huh?"

Before I could reply he fainted.

While Lucy and the children tended to Nat, I kept a watchful eye outside, worried sick about Wishbone. From time to time, I spotted Comanches moving about in the barn, but I knew they were waiting for one of us to grow careless and stick his head out.

Lucy came to my side, her forehead wrinkled with worry, but her eyes filled with determination. "What do you think they'll do now?"

I turned back to the gun port. "They can't burn us out yet. The roof's still wet, but the Comanche and Kiowa are a patient enemy. They wouldn't mind waiting two or three days until the roof dries and then burn us out."

She gasped.

I smiled at her. "They don't have us yet. And you can't tell, they might just up and decide we're not worth the bother. I've seen them do some mighty puzzling things."

"Isn't there anything we can do now?"

"Just wait. That's the hardest part, the waiting."

The day passed slowly, the sun beaming down, heating the inside of the house uncomfortably. Mid-afternoon, Nat came around. After a bellyful of warm beef broth and a tin cup of sixshooter coffee, he perked up some.

Throughout the interminable day, my gaze kept going back to the barn and Wishbone. I'd never had a great number of friends among the white man but he was one. What in the blazes had happened to him? I grimaced in despair.

Not long before dark, Lucy came to sit by me. "See anything?"

I shook my head.

She remained silent for several moments, then cleared her throat. "Didn't you say there were Kiowa with the Comanche out there?"

"Yes."

"But, didn't you say that you—"

"Lived with the Kiowa. Yes. What you need to try to understand is that the Indian is just like the white. Most obey their own laws, but there are always those like the ones out there who turn renegade. The white man has his renegades. Turncoats, traitors out for money like William Quantrell."

She studied me intently, the puzzled frown on her forehead evidence that she was considering my words.

Just before dark, a wild whooping came from the corral. I looked out a gun port and silhouetted against the setting sun, a rider astride an Indian pony raced toward the cabin. I couldn't believe my eyes. No Comanche in his right mind would try a frontal attack.

I tightened my finger on the trigger, and then shouts and gunfire from the barn froze me. I peered into the sun, then recognized the way the rider sat in the saddle. Wishbone!

"Throw that blasted door open!" he shouted.

"Quick! The door!" I yelled over my shoulder while I pumped several rounds of lead into the barn, driving the Comanche back inside.

The next moment, boots clomped in and the door slammed behind them.

"Whooee," the bow-legged cowpoke exclaimed, holding out a shirtsleeve with a bullet hole in it. "That was close."

I kept watch while Wishbone put himself around a plate of beans and several cups of coffee. He had hidden under the hay in the loft. The Comanche had gathered at one end of the barn. "Counted ten out there. From what I could see, I figured there was about forty of them old boys scattered around us." He paused and gulped down another mouthful of beans. "Anyway, when I saw my chance, I grabbed me an Injun pony and headed for the cabin. I run over two Comanche who tried to stop me," he added with a smug grin.

"Yeah," Nat said. "But what would you have done if them heathens had set the barn on fire?"

The redheaded cowpoke arched an eyebrow and ran his fingers through his curly hair. "I don't rightly know, but I reckon I would have figured out something. Ain't no redstick going to lay his hand on this hair."

As darkness crept over the Llano River Valley, I muttered, "I don't figure they'll try nothing tonight. They reckon it's just a matter of time before they got us. They can afford to be patient." But we can't, I reminded myself.

By now, two blazing fires burned on upriver and downriver banks. Dark shapes moved back and forth in front of the leaping flames that cast eerie shadows on the thick stands of cane along the shore. Behind us, two more fires burned. They had us close-herded good and proper.

Lucy was in the bedroom putting Callie to bed. Ben and Nat were at the window in the bedroom. I watched the front window, and Wishbone the rear. He whispered in the darkness, "You know we got to do something tonight, don't you, JC?"

"Yep."

"Anything in mind?"

I studied the starlight dimly illuminating the river flowing past. From time to time, darker objects—fallen trees and thick logs—floated by. "Yep." I peered up at the sky. "Be easier if we could get us some clouds."

Several moments of silence passed. Impatiently, Wishbone asked, "Well? You going to make me guess?"

"There's still some Army down at the fort. We got to get to them."

He snorted. "Well, partner. Unless you done learned how to fly, you might as well forget that idea. Ain't no way you can get through those red heathens out there. They're packed tighter than ten cowpokes on the same bunk."

"You got any notions?"

With a long sigh, he grunted, "Nope."

"Then I reckon we'll have to try it my way."

"Which way is that?"

"Underwater."

"Underwater? And just how do you figure on doing that? Breathe underwater?"

I grinned, "Yep."

In the darkness, Lucy gasped.

How long she had been listening or how much she heard, I didn't ask. I just kept watching the movement around the fires outside.

Chapter Twenty-three

I kept my eyes on the starry heavens. I had to make my move before sunrise even if I didn't get any clouds.

According to the Big Dipper, it was around four o'clock. Still no clouds. I muttered a curse. I had no choice. I had to take a chance. I whispered, "It's time. Get the door for me, Wishbone."

Suddenly, Lucy's slender fingers touched my arm. They felt like fire. "Be careful, JC. We need you," she whispered.

I grinned at her. "I'll be back."

I crept across the room to the door, which Wishbone opened for me. I paused before crawling out and leaned close to him. "If worse comes to worse, you know what to do."

He hesitated. In a strained voice, he said, "Yeah. I'll save enough cartridges." His fingers gripped my arm. "Good luck."

Suddenly, the night grew darker. Clouds were moving in. I crouched in the shadows cast by the porch until another bank of clouds rolled past.

I moved slowly, pausing as stars emerged, then moving once again as they slid behind the clouds. A man sees that which is familiar to him, Comanche included. And I was gambling they were so confident that if they had any sentries out, the guards would not be paying much attention to detail.

On my belly, I eased across the hardpan to the corral, pausing in the thin shadows cast by the pole rails. I strained my ears, but no sound came from the barn.

Quickly, I eased along the corral and into the forest where I studied the darkness around me intently. Now I had an entirely different problem. The darkness was so complete beneath the canopy of leaves, the Comanche couldn't see me, and I couldn't see them. For all I knew, they could have stationed braves every few feet surrounding the cabin. I didn't think so, but I couldn't take a chance on stumbling over one.

I lay motionless next to the trunk of a thick liveoak, waiting for sunrise. Slowly, vague shapes began to emerge in the darkness before me as false dawn eased through the forest. As soon as I could discern contours, I moved deeper into the woods.

Once, I froze as guttural voices sounded behind me. I dared not look, fearful any motion would attract their attention. I tried to force my body into the ground.

The voices passed. When they died away I continued. After a quarter of a mile I angled back to the river. By now, the outlines of trees had taken shape.

Upon reaching the river, I headed upstream, searching for the right log. Then I spotted it, fifteen to twenty feet long with a ball of roots and a trunk a couple feet thick. It had run aground by a canebrake.

Glancing up and down the river and seeing no one, I waded into the river and quickly tied two loose loops of rope around the trunk about five feet apart, loose enough for me to slip between them and the trunk. Hastily, I broke a thin stalk of hollow cane and trimmed it to about three feet.

My plan was to float beneath the log, one rope supporting my feet, the other my shoulders, and head underwater while I breathed through the hollow cane.

While I had mastered the trick as a youth, that had been over twenty years earlier. Still, it was the only chance to float past the Comanche unseen.

I pushed the log into the river. Holding on to the ball of roots, I slipped through the first loop and then hooked my feet in the second. I ran the cane up through the roots, and then taking a deep breath, submerged, using the hollow cane to breathe.

The current caught the tree, and we began to move faster.

Being more buoyant than the tree, I pressed my toes and my hands against the heavy trunk, forcing my body against the ropes so I could stay underwater. Such an effort put excruciating strain on my muscles, which I tried to block by counting to a hundred, and then a thousand.

Each time I felt I couldn't hold on, I remembered Lucy, and the thought of her and the children gave me additional strength.

Through the still muddy water, the sky grew lighter.

Finally, after what seemed like days, I lifted my head above the surface and grinned. I was well below the Comanche encampment.

An hour later, I rode beside a young lieutenant at the head of a platoon of cavalry in a brisk canter, saving the remounts for the charge.

Two miles before we reached the ranch, pops of gunfire echoed through the woods. Behind me, soldiers muttered. The lieutenant held up his hand and called over his shoulder, "Steady, men. Not yet. Another mile. Hold 'em steady, hold 'em steady."

After what seemed like hours, he rose in his stirrups and waved his Remington sixgun and shouted, "Charge!"

Waving their Sharps' rifles over their heads, the cavalrymen gave yells every bit as chilling as the old Johnny Reb scream.

* * *

We caught the Comanche by surprise. When we burst out of the forest, they were milling about, trying to regroup to hold us off, but our momentum carried us over them like a boulder rolling down hill.

Indian ponies scattered in every direction, many without riders.

A Kiowa warrior astride a roan mustang bared his teeth and charged me, his battle axe high above his head. I jerked my sixgun up and the hammer clicked on a spent cartridge. Suddenly, the warrior yanked his pony to a sliding halt, stared at me, then wheeled about and disappeared into the forest.

I breathed a sigh of relief, puzzling over why he halted his attack so abruptly.

Nat and Wishbone ran out on the porch, firing steadily at the wraithlike Indians disappearing into the forest.

The fight was brief, lasting not even five minutes, but almost a dozen Comanche lay sprawled in the mud.

I reined up to the porch as Lucy emerged from the cabin. Her eyes brightened when she saw me, and a weary smile of relief played over her lips.

I swallowed the lump in my throat. "Are you and the kids all right?"

She nodded, tears glistening in her eyes. "Fine. We're just fine now."

I studied her for several long moments, knowing the feelings I had for her were much more intense than those I had for Damita Fidelia Corina. "Good," was all I could say.

The next few weeks passed without incident until one afternoon, Ben came boiling in on his mustang, his eyes wide with excitement. "JC, JC! There's a dead Indian up by the bend in the river. Someone shot him in the back."

Wishbone and I rode out to get a handle on what might be taking place. We spotted the Indian face down at the river's edge, the water lapping at his out-thrown arm.

I shucked my sixgun and dismounted. "Keep a gun on him. He might be playing possum."

The still body did not respond when I nudged him with the toe of my boot.

"He dead?"

There was an almost imperceptible rising and falling of his back. I frowned. "I don't think so. Get ready." Using the toe of my boot, I turned the limp body over and frowned. The unconscious Indian looked familiar, and then I recognized him as my Kiowa brother, Red Eagle.

Quickly, I holstered my sixgun and dropped to my knees. "Toss me your canteen, hurry." I lifted Red Eagle's head. His bare skin burned with fever. Sweat beaded on his thin face.

Wishbone stammered, surprised by my behavior. "What the—"

I gestured impatiently. "Your canteen. Toss it to me. This is Red Eagle, my Kiowa brother."

After managing to get a few swallows of water in Red Eagle, I helped him into my saddle and held him upright until we reached the ranch. During the ride, Wishbone peppered me with dozens of questions, none of which I could answer.

With Wishbone's help, we carried Red Eagle into the bunkhouse and placed him on my bunk. I cleaned the wound, which appeared a few days old. I mixed up some monkey flower and powdered cottonwood bark to heal the wound, and forced a cup of willow root tea down his throat for fever.

As he took the last of the tea, Lucy stepped into the bunkhouse, followed by Ben and Callie.

She came to my side. With a trace of disbelief and suspicion, she whispered, "That's your brother?"

"Yes," I muttered softly.

I could feel the tension building. I waited for her to speak. Finally, in a hard, cold voice, she asked, "Was he one of those who attacked us?"

Studying Red Eagle's slumbering face, I shook my head slowly. "I can't believe he was part of it." Part of me struggled with the idea that he had taken an active role in the attack. Another part resisted such an outrageous suggestion. I looked up into her eyes.

"I don't know. If he did, he isn't the brother I grew up with."

For the time being, that seemed to satisfy her. "What do you plan to do with him?"

I shrugged. "Get him whole. Then find out what's going on." With a deep sigh, I added, "I've seen too many folk hurt for no reason when suspicious jaspers jump to conclusions before they have their facts."

She studied me a moment. "I trust you, JC. I trust you to take care of my children, to help us be safe. I'm mighty leery of that Injun"—she looked me straight in the eye—"but I trust you to do the right thing."

I met her gaze. "I'll do what I've got to do."

For another moment, her eyes stayed fixed on mine, then she nodded. "I know." She looked around. "Come on, children. Let's get back to the cabin."

"One other thing," I said.

She paused and looked around, an eyebrow arched.

"I don't know how Nat's going to feel about Red Eagle out here. Reckon if it puts a burr under his saddle, can he throw his soogan by the fireplace in the cabin?"

A knowing smile played over her lips. "You know he can."

My eyes remained on the door after she and the children left the bunkhouse. Despite her agreeable demeanor, a sense of suspicion and reservation remained behind, an awareness as palpable as the odor of a skunk.

Chapter Twenty-four

Young Nat Gallatin exploded when he came in and saw Red Eagle unconscious in my bunk. I explained the situation.

The young man glared at me. "Not me. The redstick goes. I ain't staying in no place stunk up by one of them heathens. No disrespect meant, JC, but there ain't no way I'll have nothing to do with a murdering redskin."

I held up my hand. "No disrespect taken, Nat. Mrs. Coulter said you could throw your soogan by the fire at the cabin if you wanted."

He stared at me in disbelief. His face grew red. "You mean, you're keeping that redstick here and telling me I got to move?"

"I'm not telling you to move. You're the one doing the telling. This here is my brother. Until I find out what he's up to, I'm going to treat him like my brother. And I'd have no respect for you if you didn't do the same for your own kin."

The young man studied me for several moments. His face softened. "Reckon I understand what you're saying, JC. I don't know how much I agree with it but I understand." He glanced toward the cabin and blew out a long breath between his pursed lips. "Well, I don't reckon I'll bother Miz Coulter to sleep up there tonight."

It was still dark next morning when I felt a hand on my shoulder shaking me awake. I looked up from where I was sleeping on the floor beside my bunk. Red Eagle was staring down at me. I sat up abruptly.

"You sleep hard," he whispered. "Too much time with the white man."

Rising quickly, I stoked the banked fire and put coffee on to boil. By the time I poured the first cups, Nat and Wishbone had awakened.

Sitting up in my bunk, Red Eagle studied them suspiciously but I put him to ease. "They're good friends." I hooked my index fingers across my chest, the southern tribes' sign language for friendship. "Good friends just like you and me are brothers."

He nodded to them. "That is good." He winced.

I checked his wound. It was healing, but seepage had stained the bandage. While Nat and Wishbone looked on, I worked up a fresh mixture of powdered cottonwood bark and monkey flower. Red Eagle's fever had broken so I skipped the willow root tea.

"Now, tell me, brother," I said, leaning back and pulling out a bag of Bull Durham. "Who shot you? Why are you here?"

He glanced suspiciously at Nat and Wishbone, then explained. "I am ashamed to tell you, brother, but I know of the *renegados* who attack your *rancheria*. One was Tall Wolf."

In a flash of understanding, I remembered the Kiowa warrior who had abruptly aborted his attack on me. "Yes. I know Tall Wolf."

"It was from him I learn you are here." He glanced warily at my two compadres, then continued. "His followers are those who shot me. When he told me of seeing you, I knew I must come to warn you. He forbid me but I slipped away. For several days, I kept his men at bay." He grinned. "They are poor readers of sign, poor enough to be easily fooled." He grew serious. "But, not too foolish. Two days ago, three of them find me. I kill them, but not before one shot me."

I nodded. "Our father has much to be proud with you, my brother. Now, why the urgency to see me?"

"I come to warn you. There is much unrest in the tribes. The white man has broken many treaties. He has murdered women and children. The tribes are angry and seek revenge."

I stiffened. My blood grew cold. "And you, Red Eagle. Do you feel the same?"

He shook his head. "No. When our father died, I knew I should strive for peace as he. The Indian cannot defeat the white man." He glanced at Wishbone and Nat, then continued. "To try to do so is foolish. We must have peace. That is why I come. Many Kiowa and Comanche led by Black Buffalo have joined with white renegades. They plan to grow rich by burning and destroying settlements west of Austin and San Antonio, all the way down to the great waters beyond." He paused. "That is why I come. They are many, so many I believe they can kill all of the bluecoats who try to defend you."

I drew a deep breath and released it slowly. "Where are they now?"

Red Eagle shrugged. "All I know is they come here."

Wishbone spoke up, his voice edged with suspicion. "How do you know that?"

"I hear them. I hear the one called Wingo speak to a man of you, my brother. Of this place on the river." He paused and sheepishly added, "I cannot say of what they spoke for they moved away from me. That is how I know where to find you."

Nat muttered a soft curse.

Wishbone cursed. "Blast that Wingo. I always figured he was no good."

My mind leaped forward. "This jasper Wingo spoke with. What did he look like?" I held my breath.

Red Eagle considered my question a moment. He held his open hand under his chin. "Big jaw, eyes like the snake. He does not stand as high as you."

I hissed through clenched teeth. "Hugh Garrett!"

Wishbone looked up at me in surprise. "You think so? It's him? I can't believe it."

I nodded slowly. "Close-set eyes, big jaw. If it isn't him, it's his twin."

That night around the supper table in the cabin, we discussed the chilling revelations of Red Eagle.

"Do you believe him?" asked Lucy.

"He's my brother. He wouldn't lie. Not to me. Besides, how would he know Wingo's name? I don't know how many are coming, but I reckon we can plan on getting hit again."

She nodded. "Then what do we do?"

"First, in the morning, we'll pack you and the kids up and ride into the fort. Captain Irwin needs to meet Red Eagle and hear what he has to say."

Lucy glanced around the cabin. "Leave here? But—"

"For the time being. Until all this is settled. We can work better knowing you and the kids are safe."

Reluctantly, she agreed.

Little Ben spoke up. "But, I can help. I can fight."

I shook my head. "I need someone to take care of your mother and sister."

He ducked his head and frowned.

"Someone I can depend on, Ben. That's you."

With a shy grin, he looked up and nodded. "If you say so."

*   *   *

Captain Irwin arched a skeptical eyebrow as he listened to Red Eagle, informing me afterward that he didn't believe the story, and the only reason he wasn't going to have Red Eagle hanged was because I vouched for him.

"Then why, Captain, would he put himself in such a position if the story wasn't true? If he was part of it, he wouldn't be here warning us. What would he have to gain by that?"

"Maybe he's trying to mislead us, get us away from the fort." He shook his head slowly. "Those people are sneaky, Thornton. You ought to know that having lived with them."

Talking to the captain was like preaching to an outhouse.

"At least, put Mrs. Coulter and the children up until we see what is going on."

He nodded emphatically. "By all means. I still think it's a trick of some sort, but I'm more than willing to accommodate Mrs. Coulter. The officers' quarters all have private entrances. We have some spare rooms there."

Red Eagle remained in the saddle of his pony while we moved Lucy and the children into a clean room adjoining the officers' quarters.

She laid her hand on my arm when I turned to leave. "Be careful, JC."

I laid my gnarled hand on hers. "Nothing to worry about. Nothing at all," I replied with a heap more confidence than I felt.

Chapter Twenty-five

I swung into the saddle and looked over at young Nat. Given the boy's size, no one would have taken him for fifteen. In the last year, he'd put on another thirty pounds and three inches. He was man-sized. "You don't have to go, Nat. Maybe it's best you stay here and look after Mrs. Coulter and the kids."

He eyed me unsteadily, then glanced at Wishbone and Red Eagle. "That ranch is the only home I've ever knowed, JC." He paused to chew on his bottom lip. "I reckon I wouldn't be much of a man if I didn't stand up and fight for it."

If he'd been my own son I couldn't have been prouder of the boy—maybe I should say the young man because he no longer acted like a boy. I nodded. "Good enough."

As we rode away from the officers' quarters, Captain

Irwin emerged from headquarters and came out to meet us. "What are your plans, Thornton?"

I ran my finger along the scar on my cheekbone thoughtfully. "I reckon a couple of us will do a little reconnoitering."

He cut his eyes to Wishbone and Nat. "What about the others?"

I grinned and nodded to the general store. "They'll be busy working up a surprise for the bunch after I make a stop over there."

While Wishbone and Nat waited with Red Eagle, I went inside and bought a case of dynamite.

Both cowpokes frowned when I returned and lashed it behind my saddle.

As I swung into the saddle, Wishbone asked, "What's with the dynamite?"

I grinned. "A surprise."

Nat's frown deepened. "What kind of surprise?"

With a click of my tongue, I sent my pony down the road. "You know that box canyon with the trail in back leading up to the rim?"

"I know it," Nat replied. "About a mile from where we pen our cattle in that other canyon."

I scooted around in the saddle and looked at them. "Red Eagle and me are going to hit the renegades before they attack the cabin. They'll follow us. We'll lead them into the canyon. Once they're inside, you blow the mouth shut."

Wishbone chuckled. "That's a dandy idea, JC. Sure wish I'd thought of that."

Nat frowned. "But, what about you and"—he cut his eyes to Red Eagle—"and him?"

"We'll be heading up to the rim. With one of you on either side, as soon as you blow the mouth, give us a few minutes, then blow the walls."

Wishbone drawled. "What if we don't get them all?"

I arched an eyebrow. "I don't figure we will, but we can carve a big notch out of their little party."

"Them left alive is going to be spitting mad."

Pursing my lips, I nodded. "I figure they will. That's why, we need to pen the stock in the east canyon and throw our gear in the caves there. There's where we can hole up."

"Sounds good to me," Wishbone said.

"Me too," echoed Nat.

When we rode up to the cabin a couple of hours later, I nodded to Wishbone. "You and Nat carry the dynamite out to the box canyon. Red Eagle and me will load up our gear and cache it in the caves when we pen the stock in the other canyon. Then we'll ride over and give you a hand."

After the two rode away, I looked hard at Red Eagle. "How are you feeling? You up to some more riding?"

I saw the pain in his eyes when he grunted and replied, "The wound is healing. I can ride."

By mid-afternoon, we had pushed the twenty head of

cattle and ten mules into the box canyon and stowed our gear in the caves. Then we turned back west to the trap we were laying for Garrett and Wingo.

"We've fused the dynamite," announced Wishbone as he pointed out the fissures in the rocky strata down which they planned to drop the sticks.

"We cached the dynamite on either side of the canyon out of the weather. It won't take us five minutes to pull them out, unwrap them, and set 'em off," a beaming Nat explained.

I grinned at both of them. "Looks like we're ready. Now, it's up to Red Eagle and me."

I rode out that night. After a few miles, I began casting about in a broad circle, sniffing for the odor of wood smoke, peering into the night for flashes of fire.

To the east, false dawn lit the sky dimly. I was riding over unfamiliar country when I ran upon a granite wall three hundred feet high and about a quarter of a mile wide. An overhang of jagged gray granite jutted from the top of the wall.

Moving slowly, I circled to the rear of the liveoak-dotted ridge and made my way to the top. I grinned to myself when I reached the overhang. It was the perfect spot for us to keep an eye on the countryside. From there, we could see Garrett and Wingo while they were still ten miles distant.

Back south, a thin ribbon of silver twisted through the rolling countryside. The Llano. I followed its tortuous course east, orienting myself as to the ranch's location.

Two days passed without incident. Two days of uncertainty, of wondering if I was doing the right thing, or if there was a better way of taking care of Garrett. I had no doubt Red Eagle heard what he reported, but I was also beginning to wonder if perhaps Wingo and Garrett had changed their plans.

Mid-afternoon on the third day, Nat came boiling down from the overhang. "They're coming, they're coming!" he shouted. We ran out to meet him. "About thirty more or less, Injun and white. Back west. Looks like they plan to hit the river near Silver Creek in about an hour or so."

The restiveness plaguing me the last few days vanished, replaced with a sense of purpose. "Good job, Nat." I looked at Wishbone. "You know what to do. Get up there and plant those charges. You'll hear the gunfire, and then see us when we hit the canyon. Wait until they get in."

Nat gulped and nodded. "That's cutting it awful close, JC."

I winked at him. "You can do it."

After Nat and Wishbone disappeared into the forest north of the cabin, I swung into my saddle and reined my black stallion around. Studying the river, I said, "I reckon we'll follow the shore until we spot them."

Red Eagle grunted.

I grinned at him. "Remember, brother. If either of us goes down, the other keeps going. We've got to get those jaspers in that canyon."

"I remember." He grinned. "Don't you forget, my brother."

With a click of my tongue, I sent Pedro trotting along the river's edge. I glanced at the sun. "Silver Creek's about an hour. We got plenty of daylight to get the job done."

Maybe fifteen minutes later, Red Eagle reined up abruptly. I followed his lead. He peered into the forest ahead, his head cocked to one side, listening intently, his face a mask of concentration. Suddenly the mask contorted into a savage grin. He looked at me and pointed into the shadows beneath the canopy of oak and hickory leaves.

I nodded, wondering if he was mistaken. I figured it would be another thirty minutes or so before we confronted the renegades. I sat motionless, listening. I couldn't hear a sound other than the calls of the blue-jay and the copycat whistling of the mockingbird. Suddenly the birds grew silent, having heard the same sounds as Red Eagle.

Pointing to the ground, I indicated we were to remain

here. Let Wingo and Garrett come to us. I shucked my Colt, checked the cartridges, holstered it, then slipped my Yellowboy Henry from the boot. I wanted my first few shots to serve up a warning the renegades couldn't ignore.

Suddenly voices mixed with the click of metal against metal drifted through the forest, growing louder by the minute. I glanced at Red Eagle. He held his carbine ready.

In the distance, I saw movement. "Not yet," I whispered. "We must be certain it's Wingo and Garrett."

Red Eagle frowned. "Who else could it be?"

I shrugged. "We've got to be sure." I eased the Henry to my shoulder and whispered, "If it's them, make the first two or three count."

He chuckled. "Do not caution me, brother. You are the one to make certain."

I just grinned and lined up the sight on the rider of the first pony, a white man. "Ready?" I whispered.

"Ready."

We waited another few moments until we could make out a half dozen riders. My eyes narrowed as I recognized George Wingo as the jasper I had my sights on. They had not seen us for we remained motionless in the thick growth of oak and hickory, but as soon as we moved, they'd spot us.

I tightened my finger on the trigger. "Now," I said through dry lips.

My Henry boomed, its deafening roar bouncing off

the trees in the closed confines of the forest. At the same moment I squeezed the trigger Wingo's horse shied, and my slug caught the second cowpoke. He shot backward from his saddle, like a great fist had struck him in the chest.

We touched off another three or four shots before wheeling about and racing through the forest. Wild shouts of pursuit echoed above the screeching melee of confused yelling and cries of pain.

We angled toward the shore, but remained just inside the tree line so we wouldn't present as much of a target. Shots exploded from behind, and slugs thumped into tree trunks, ripping away chunks of bark, revealing the white wood below.

Our ponies weaved in and out through the trees. I ducked to avoid a low hanging limb. Then Red Eagle gestured north. Time to turn and head for the canyon.

We burst out of the forest and into the valley leading to the canyon. Another mile.

Suddenly, Red Eagle's roan whinnied and collapsed on its front legs. Reacting instantly, the Kiowa warrior leaped from the saddle, landing on his feet, but his momentum sent him tumbling head over heels. He jumped to his feet and waved me on.

Ignoring my earlier orders, I wheeled Pedro about and raced back to him. By now a cluster of white and Indian riders had emerged from the forest and were thundering across the valley about a quarter of a mile behind.

Leaning from my saddle, I extended my arm as I

wheeled the black stallion in a tight circle around Red Eagle, who seized my arm and lithely swung on to the rump of my horse.

By now, the whizzing slugs were getting too close. Chunks of soil exploded in front of us. I clenched my teeth and dug my spurs into Pedro's flanks. The big stallion leaped forward, almost flying.

Moments later, we raced through the mouth of the canyon and vanished back in the thick stands of cedar filling the canyon.

I waited, expecting a deafening explosion at any moment. Could something have gone wrong? No, not to both Nat and Wishbone.

But, what if—

And then two booming explosions settled my concerns.

Chapter Twenty-six

At the rear of the canyon, we leaped from the back of
the stallion. Red Eagle stumbled when he hit the ground.
I looked around. His wound had opened. Blood ran
down his bare chest and dripped onto his muscular thigh.

Despite his protests, I put him back in the saddle and
led Pedro up the steep and narrow trail to the rim. Behind us, wild shots and frightened shouts echoed off the
canyon walls, a strident cacophony of jarring sounds.

We were halfway up to the rim when four more explosions rocked the canyon. I felt the rocky trail beneath my feet tremble. I hoped the trail held. I urged
Pedro to move faster.

Finally, we topped out on the rim.

I looked into the canyon. Great boulders and gigantic
shards of granite covered the canyon floor. I saw no

movement. I nodded in satisfaction. We did what we started out to do. I couldn't help wondering if Wingo and Garrett were beneath the layers of rock. If Garrett was, then I could forget about ever clearing my name.

I turned to Red Eagle, but he sat slumped in the saddle, his chin on his chest. Quickly, I lowered him to the ground and removed my neckerchief and doused the wound with water from my canteen.

By the time Nat and Wishbone reached us, I'd stopped the bleeding and was administering a fresh layer of monkey flower and cottonwood bark to the wound.

During the short ride to the cave in the east canyon, Wishbone and Nat figured at least a dozen riders had followed us into the canyon, some white, some Indian. "That still leaves fifteen to twenty," Nat added.

Wishbone and I rode out, leaving Nat and Red Eagle in the cave. "We'll take a look at the ranch, see what's happening there."

Suddenly, smoke rose above the treetops in the direction of the ranch. Wishbone cursed. "I hope that ain't what I think," he growled.

I grimaced. "I don't know what else it could be."

We rode warily, staying away from the occasional clearings in the forest. By now, the smell of smoke permeated the woods. "Over there," I muttered, nodding to the humpback ridge that shouldered its way above the treetops.

Reining up in a narrow grotto that cut through the ridge, we climbed the jumble of boulders to the crest where we could view the ranch.

My blood ran cold when I saw flames leaping from the barn and roof of the cabin. Even as we watched, the barn collapsed on itself, sending a column of fiery sparks billowing a hundred feet into the air.

Wishbone shook my arm and gasped. "JC. Look! Down by the river. That's little Ben! And that's Wingo."

I frantically scanned the several small groups along the shore until I spotted Ben struggling to break free of the grip Wingo had on his arm.

The young boy kicked and swung his free arm, but Wingo and the others just laughed. Then I spotted Hugh Garrett, who strode forward and slapped Ben across the face, knocking the boy to the ground where he lay unmoving.

Garrett gestured to one of the nearby Comanches, indicating he was to throw the boy on a pony. I muttered a curse. Garrett had turned Comanchero. That no-account vermin was planning on selling the boy down in Mexico.

I backed away hastily. "Let's git."

Wishbone grunted and followed. "What are we going to do? They's too many of them for just the two of us."

My mind raced, too occupied searching for a plan to pay attention to the forest below. As we clambered over the jagged boulders descending the ridge, a powerful blow hit my leg, knocking it from under me and sending me tumbling from the boulder down into a narrow crevice as the report of the rifle echoed up the ridge.

I heard a second shot, and then the back of my head exploded, and darkness engulfed me.

The pounding in the back of my head awakened me. When I opened my eyes, I could see nothing. I blinked. Still complete darkness. I lay motionless, staring into the darkness for several moments, trying to remember where I was. My thoughts were jumbled.

I could see nothing, just a black emptiness. I moved my hand in front of my eyes and blinked. Still nothing. Blind!

Then I felt the throbbing in my leg. I moved my hand to my thigh, feeling the wound. The leg of my trousers was soggy with blood. I tried moving my leg, sighing with relief when I discovered the slug had broken no bones. I felt the inside of my thigh. It seemed no soggier than the outside, which meant the lead had missed the big artery.

I closed my eyes and tried to relax as an oppressive wave of lassitude rolled over me. At least I would live even If I was blind.

Splatters of water spraying my face awakened me. When I opened my eyes, I had to stifle a shout of joy. Overhead, daylight shone around the edges of a granite overhang under which I lay. Water dripped from the overhang from rain.

The bleeding from the wound had subsided, but the pain persisted. Clenching my teeth, I struggled to sit. I reached for my neckerchief and remembered I'd used it to patch up Red Eagle. I tore a strip from the bottom of my shirt and tied it tightly around the wound.

Moving slowly so as not to reawaken the throbbing in my head, I looked around for a way out.

The slab on which I lay slanted to a box-shaped opening several feet below. I crawled on my hands and one knee, dragging the injured leg after me.

I paused at the mouth, searching the ridge around me and the forest several yards distant. I saw no movement, so I silently slipped out and in the rain managed to stumble to the welcome shadows of the oak and hickory forest.

It was almost dark when I hobbled into the cave back in the box canyon.

"JC!" Nat rushed to meet me and help me deep into the cave. Questions tumbled from his lips.

I glanced at Red Eagle who was sitting up, leaning against the wall of the cave. When he saw the bandage about my leg, he grunted and climbed to his feet.

While Nat poured me a cup of coffee, Red Eagle tended to my wound. The walk from the ridge opened it some, but he quickly staunched what little flow there was. He tossed me a peyote petal. "Eat."

Nat babbled. "What happened? We thought you was dead or something. You been gone two days. Is Wishbone with you?"

I shook my head and told them what I remembered.

When I finished, Red Eagle reached for his carbine and rose. "I go find the other one."

"Look for the boy too. He's out there."

Red Eagle's eyes narrowed. "I find."

Nat frowned. "But it's dark."

He grinned. "The rain stops. There is a full moon tonight."

I drew a deep breath. "Take care. Those yahoos might still be around."

The fire and peyote relaxed my tense muscles, and the hot coffee warmed my belly. I nodded to the flames dancing in the small fire. "Wasn't you fearful someone would smell the smoke?"

Nat shook his head and indicated water dripping from the cave roof a few feet deeper in the cave. "It goes out there. I figure by the time it reaches the rim, and the wind up there catches it, there ain't nothing left to smell."

When Red Eagle did not return before dawn, I grew concerned. Doubts and questions filled my head. Were Garrett and Wingo still around? Had they captured Red Eagle, or worse yet, killed him?

I breathed a sigh of relief when he returned just before noon, but that relief was shattered by the stunning announcement that Wishbone was dead.

Red Eagle held up two fingers. "Shot this many

times. Rain washed away most sign, but enough was left to see they head back west."

One further question was on my mind, one I hated to ask but knew I must. "Any sign of the boy?"

Solemnly, Red Eagle shook his head.

Nat cursed. "I hope them red heathens don't hurt the sprout before they sell him to the Mexicans."

If Nat's blasphemy of the red man bothered Red Eagle, he gave no indication. "It could be, my brother, they will do with him as our father did with you."

Nat frowned. "What does he mean by that, JC?"

"Sometimes Indians—Kiowa, Comanche, Apache—they sometimes take in children to replace those they lost. Red Eagle here had an older brother, Little Otter, who was killed. After my folks was killed, the Kiowa took me in and raised me in the place of Little Otter. That's what he's talking about."

The frown on Nat's forehead deepened. "You're saying that the Kiowa killed your folks, then took you in?"

I nodded. "That's about the size of it."

He glared murderously at Red Eagle, who had squatted and was pouring himself a cup of coffee nonchalantly. "But, how could you live with them knowing they'd killed your folks?"

I studied young Nat, knowing he'd probably not understand, at least not for a few more years. "I didn't know right away. I was twelve when I left with the professor. That's when Big Horse, my Kiowa father, told me. By then, I was part of them. They had treated me decent, just like one of their own. Maybe it's hard for us to understand some of their beliefs, but I promise you," I said with a chuckle, "it's a heap harder for them to understand some of our beliefs."

"But—but it never bothered you none?"

"Oh, there was a time when I was fifteen or sixteen and full of vim and vinegar that it bothered me. But the professor helped me understand that you don't blame one red man for what another does just like you don't blame me for what Wingo has gone and done."

Nat pondered my explanation. He shook his head. "Still, I don't know. Something just don't seem right about it."

Red Eagle spoke up. "Our people have a wise medicine man who goes by the name of Skywalker. He cautions all young boys to live the life of enemies before he truly accepts them as such."

The young man frowned. "I don't understand what you mean."

"You will, Nat," I replied. "One of these days, you will."

Chapter Twenty-seven

When I broke the horrifying news to Lucy in her quarters at the fort, she closed her eyes and an anguished moan came from deep in her slender throat. She swayed slightly. I reached for her, but she steadied herself and opened her eyes. In a strained but controlled voice she mumbled, "He slipped away before I knew. I guess he wanted to help you." She hesitated. "Do you think you can find him, JC?" She cut her eyes at Red Eagle, then back to me. "You and Red Eagle?"

I smiled reassuringly. "We'll bring him back to you, Lucy. That I promise." I looked down at Callie who was clinging to her mother's leg, her eyes wide with fear. I clenched my teeth against the pain in my leg. "Don't you worry, Callie. Your brother's coming back."

Leaving Lucy and Callie at the fort, Red Eagle and I

rode out with Nat accompanying us. He had insisted, and so, against my better judgment, I gave in, hoping I wouldn't regret letting the young man ride with us.

Despite the rain, sign left by twenty shod and unshod ponies was easy to follow at a fast pace. Mid-afternoon, we crossed the Llano and picked up the trail on the other side. It was heading south now. We followed until sunset and made a cold camp in the middle of a ring of jagged boulders. I figured we'd made about thirty miles or so.

I sighed with relief as I rested my leg. The ride had opened the wound but I quickly stopped the flow.

The next day at mid-morning, we ran upon the remains of a deserted camp that obviously had been utilized as a holding pen for captured women and children bound for bondage in Mexico. Red Eagle studied it for several moments then swung into his saddle. "Two nights," he said.

Massaging my leg, I studied the sign. "They picked up five or six of their own vermin here. From the sign, they're carrying eight or ten captives not counting the boy."

Nat frowned. "Where do you reckon they're heading?"

"Got no idea. We keep following and keep pushing."

Red Eagle pointed south. "There is talk of a settlement on the river they call the Frio. Many miles from Fort Wood."

His words jogged my memories of years past. "From

Wood, they can cut across the prairie to Nuevo Negras on the Mexico side of the Rio Grande." I looked at Red Eagle. "Is Nuevo Negras still a Comanchero stronghold?"

His bronze face grew hard. He nodded tersely. "Yes."

Studying the trail, I tried to put myself in Wingo's and Garrett's heads. Chances were they planned to hit the settlement on the Frio. If I were in their shoes, after I hit the settlement, I'd head for Mexico. Sell my captives. I glanced at the sun baking down. "Forget the trail. Let's cut across for Nuevo Negras."

Red Eagle grinned but Nat frowned. "What if you're wrong? What if they're not there?"

I touched my spurs to my pony's flanks. "That's the only place around they can sell their captives. They've got to go there, and we'll be waiting."

The country from the Frio to the Rio Grande was flatter than a wet leaf. Thin gramma covered the desolate prairie that was dotted with vast stretches of almost impenetrable chaparral, thick growths of scrub oak that could hide a thousand wild longhorns.

That day, we made a slight detour north to a water hole to fill our canteens. The throbbing in my leg grew worse, forcing me to chew another petal of peyote. The second day just before dark, we spotted Nuevo Negras across the river. We reined up back in the chaparral, out of sight from any casual eyes, but where we could watch the road twisting between stands of chaparral and terminating at the river crossing. Deep in the scrub we found a water hole.

During the long ride, I'd tried to come up with a plan to confront Garrett and Wingo, but any way I played my cards, our three guns were no match for the fifteen or twenty behind Garrett.

The next few days passed slowly with no sign of Garrett or Wingo nor of any captives.

Nat and I were lazing in the shade near the water hole while Red Eagle watched the road. Overhead, storm clouds began to build, those afternoon thunderstorms fueled by the sweltering heat rising from the prairie. "Maybe they kept going south after they hit the settlement on the Frio," Nat muttered, lowering his canteen and dragging the back of his hand across his lips.

I arched an eyebrow. "Makes no difference. Here's where they'll come to sell them."

At that moment, Red Eagle rode in. He pointed east. "They come."

"How many?" I asked, leaping to my feet and throwing the saddle on my pony.

He shrugged. "Many prisoners." He held up four fingers. This many Comancheros."

I couldn't believe our luck. The Kiowa Sun god had smiled on us.

Nat frowned at me. "Where are the others?"

"The others," I explained hurriedly, "are still raiding. They sent only a handful to escort the captives to Nuevo

Negras. That's how confident they are nobody's on their trail."

"Sure hope little Ben is one of them," the young man whispered.

We reined up on the edge of the chaparral where deep ruts worn into the ground by butcher-knife wheels passed within ten feet of the thick scrub. Red Eagle nodded to the patch of scrub oak and mesquite across the road. "I go there." He slid his heavy bow from under the saddle fender.

"Good. We'll stay here." I turned to Nat. "Don't shoot off that hogleg unless you got no choice. No sense in bringing a bunch of those yahoos across the river after us."

The young man nodded.

A crash of lightning lanced through the sky to the south. My pony jittered about. The wind picked up.

Minutes passed slowly. Some hundred yards up the road, I could make out the vague outline of Red Eagle back in the chaparral, but only because I watched him ride into the thicket. To riders passing by, he was invisible.

The wind gusted harder, picking up dust and hurling it into our eyes.

And then the small party came into sight. Eleven horses were lashed single file, their riders' wrists bound to the saddle horns. Two Comancheros rode at the head of the column and two in the rear.

"Easy now. Let Red Eagle do his work. If we're lucky, we can get what we want and light a shuck back to Kimble County without a body knowing we were anywhere around."

Nat lifted an eyebrow. He gulped. His Adam's apple bobbed up and down. "Hope you're right, JC. I most certainly do."

A splash of light rain raced across the dusty road, stirring up puffs of dust. The lead Comancheros were twenty yards from us when Red Eagle quickly put yard-long arrows through the two riders bringing up the rear.

The second one let out a cry as he fell from his pony, and the two in front wheeled about. Nat and I burst from the chaparral, guns drawn, fingers tight on the triggers. "Hold on, boys. Don't go making a bad mistake," I shouted as we boiled up behind the two.

They froze.

"Drop those hoglegs." One clattered to the hardpan instantly. The other Comanchero hesitated. I growled, "Drop it, or I drop you."

The sixgun fell to the ground.

I nodded to Nat. "Tie their hands behind them, then lash their feet to the stirrups."

"JC!" I recognized Ben's voice, but I kept my eyes on the two Comancheros. "Everything's all right now, boy. We'll cut all of you loose when we finish here."

Nat stepped back. "All done."

Taking the reins of the Comancheros' ponies, I led

them to the rear of the column while Nat freed the captives—two young boys besides Ben and eight women ranging in age from early teens to late twenties. Two of the younger women broke down and cried when they realized they had been rescued.

While the older women consoled them, we dragged the dead Comancheros into the chaparral, and then, as the rain intensified, headed back to Kimble County. We rode until well after midnight, then pulled into a patch of scrub oak to rest our horses and grab a few winks for ourselves despite the rain.

During the early morning hours, the storm passed, and I informed Nat and Red Eagle I was returning to Nuevo Negras for Garrett. The two of them would have no trouble guiding the freed captives to Kimble County.

"You reckon them Comancheros will follow us?" Nat frowned.

Red Eagle shook his head. "The rain. It wipe away sign."

"He's right, Nat. They won't find nothing for twenty or thirty miles." I nodded to the Comancheros we had tied to a large mesquite. "Leave those jaspers with me. I'll take care of them."

Nat's eyes grew wide. "You mean—"

"No." I chuckled and unsaddled a Comanchero pony. "You're taking one of their ponies and their guns." I tossed the saddle on the ground. "I'll take this pony. Before I head back to Nuevo Negras, I'll turn these two jaspers loose." I grinned at the consternation in his eyes and added, "Alive."

I turned to a dozen tired and weary captives whose faces were lined with the grime of hard riding, but in each face burned eyes bright with determination. "If you ride all day and well into the night, you can reach the Llano River. Red Eagle here is my Kiowa brother. Him and this young cowboy, Nat Gallatin, are to be trusted. Follow their instructions, and this time tomorrow morning, you'll be safe." I fixed my eyes on Ben. "You do what Nat and Red Eagle say, you hear?"

Ben nodded. "I hear."

I watched until the small band disappeared into the chaparral, then turned to the Comancheros. "If I was smart, I'd shoot the two of you and leave you here for the wolves. That's what I'll do if I run into either one of you again." I cut one's hands free, then swung into the saddle and looked down at them. "Don't forget my words." I clicked my tongue and, leading the last of their ponies, headed for Nuevo Negras.

Sometime early the next morning before sun up, I crossed the Rio Grande a couple of miles above the small village.

My clothes were worn and thick with trail dust. I looked like any of the hundreds of drifters who rode in, downed a cool beer, and then drifted on.

So naturally, few eyes turned in my direction as I

reined up in front of a cantina with a portico about mid-morning. I tied my horses to the rail. I found a table on the porch and ordered coffee and beans with chilies.

A young señorita slid a bowl of steaming beans and a platter of corn tortillas on the table in front of me, then poured me a cup of coffee.

I busied myself with my meal, while at the same time my eyes searched the plaza before me.

All I can figure is that I was living right, that the Kiowa Sun god had smiled on me, for a burst of raucous laughter from across the plaza caught my attention. Squinting through the horses at the hitching rail, I spotted Hugh Garrett with his arm around the waist of a winsome señorita. He turned up a bottle of tequila and gulped half of it down before ushering her into the two-story adobe.

Chapter Twenty-eight

Growing at one end of the hitching rail was a spiny ocotillo, the tips of its branches drooping like fishhooks. I eased behind it and kept a sharp eye on the adobe. Moments later, the señorita appeared in a doorway leading to a balcony, then closed the door.

I faced a quandary. Did I take him now, or wait and risk the possibility he would leave town?

There was no choice. I had to wait. For all I knew, three quarters of the hombres, Mexican, Indians, and gringos sauntering around the small village might be part of his band of owlhoots.

Surveying the small village, I spotted a livery. What I didn't spot was the *caballero* watching me as I led my two horses into the small barn.

After graining and rubbing down my pony and the

Comanchero horse, all the while keeping a furtive watch on the two-story adobe, I shuffled lazily across the plaza to a local pulqueria for a mug of pulque, a foul-tasting drink made by fermenting the agave.

Two Mexican *caballeros* looked up when I slumped into a table at the end of the portico. At the table next to them sat a hard-bitten cowboy who appeared more interested in his whiskey than me.

Ordering a glass of pulque, I kept my eyes on the plaza, but in the periphery of my vision, I watched every movement of the *caballeros*. It wouldn't pay for them to grow too curious.

After downing the pulque, I headed back to the livery from where I watched the two Mexicans. After another few minutes, they rode out of town. I relaxed.

Squatting in the shade of the livery, I spent the remainder of the day being as invisible as I could.

Just before sundown, the door to Garrett's room opened, and he came out on the balcony with the young señorita at his side. They sat at a table and were served a sumptuous meal of half-a-dozen courses topped off with two bottles of wine.

The gay laughter of the two carried across the plaza above the local din of merriment and gaiety. I grinned to myself. Garrett and the señorita had nothing on their minds but each other.

At that moment, George Wingo lumbered onto the balcony and spoke to Garrett, who simply laughed and waved him away. Wingo stood fixed in his tracks before abruptly spinning around and disappearing back through the open door.

I had a nebulous plan in my head, one with a heap of loose ends, but I reminded myself that the game I was playing down here was full of loose ends.

Suddenly, a voice at my shoulder spun me around. "*Buenos dias*, senor."

I looked into the suspicious eyes of a *caballero*. "Howdy."

He gestured to the Comanchero pony. "I see you when you ride in this morning, señor. This animal here, I think I have seen him before."

Cursing myself for not anticipating someone who might recognize the animal, I arched an eyebrow. "Not a bad looking pony, is he, amigo? He belonged to a cowpoke I ran across about a day's ride to the north. The jasper was down on his luck so I bought this animal for a double eagle. I wouldn't mind turning a profit on him. Interested?"

The *caballero* studied me suspiciously. "No, señor, but that is hard to believe. This one, he belongs to Luiz Arredondo. He would not sell the animal."

I shrugged. "Well, it wasn't no *caballero* I got him from. It was a gringo. I don't know what took place before that."

He pursed his thin lips, then turned to inspect the pony once again. The hair on the back of my neck bristled. Suddenly, he grabbed his sixgun and spun, right into the muzzle of my Colt. He went down with a grunt.

Hastily, I tied and gagged the *caballero*, then dragged him into a rear stall and covered him with hay. I had no choice now. I had to move, and move fast.

Swinging into the saddle, I grabbed the lead rope and led the Comanchero pony from the livery. Moving slowly, I rode into the chaparral north of Nuevo Negras, then swung around, coming in to the rear of the two-story adobe.

By now the moon had risen, and to my surprise, tied to a rail at the rear of the adobe were several horses, among them Pedro. I glanced at the moon, and thanked the Kiowa gods guiding me.

Angry shouts, gay laughter, and occasional gunshots echoed from the cantina as I made my way up the back steps. I paused at the door, drew a deep breath, then slowly opened it, peering down the hall, which to my relief was empty. There were three doors on either side of the hall. The last one on the left I guessed was Garrett's

I tiptoed down the hall, expecting a door to open at any moment, but luck was with me. I paused at the closed door, listening.

Silence.

Down below, two more gunshots boomed followed by a riotous roar of risqué laughter.

Taking a deep breath, I shoved the door open and jumped inside. Garrett's face twisted in anger when he saw me. He grabbed for his sixgun but I slammed my Colt into his temple. He collapsed, and I instantly turned the muzzle on the startled señorita.

"Say nothing," I said harshly. "I won't hurt you. Understand?"

She nodded briefly.

I pointed to the bed. "Lie down."

Her eyes grew wide.

"Lie down," I hissed through clenched teeth.

Reluctantly, she did as I said, and I quickly bound and gagged her. I leaned forward and whispered in her ear. "My partner's outside on the balcony. If you leave this room in the next ten minutes, he'll shoot. Understand?"

She nodded again.

At that moment, shouts of alarm came from the livery. The *caballero* must have awakened and worked his bonds loose.

With a grunt, I threw Garrett over my shoulder and hurried back down the stairs. I winced as I started down the stairs. The extra weight on my shoulder almost made my injured leg buckle. I felt the warmth of fresh blood.

Outside, I quickly lashed him belly down over my saddle, then untied Pedro. Just before I swung into the saddle, a guttural voice called out from the darkness around the cantina. "Garrett? That you? What's going on? I thought you was up with the señorita?"

Wingo! I muttered a curse.

I peered over Pedro's neck. Wingo stood in the shadows with another dark figure.

He took a step toward me. "Garrett?" His voice grew suspicious. "Who's out there? Better answer or I'll start shooting."

I was backed into the proverbial corner, a grizzly on one side and mountain lion on the other. I shucked my sixgun.

Suddenly, half-a-dozen gunshots rang out from inside the cantina. I took a quick sidestep from under my pony's neck and fanned off two rapid shots, so close together the report sounded as one.

By the time Wingo and his partner spun to the ground, I was in the saddle and disappearing back into the chaparral with Hugh Garrett. I had at least eight hours before they could track me.

Chapter Twenty-nine

During that first day, few words passed between Garrett and me but all of them were acrimonious.

He snorted and laughed. "Sure I lied. I'd do it again, but I'll never admit it to anyone else."

I studied him. "Makes no sense. I never met you until that day with Colonel Avery."

A sneer played over his lips. "That's right. And you never knew Mack Dimmitt until you killed him either."

Mack Dimmitt! How could I forget him? "Yeah. The vermin murdered the man who raised me. He tried to kill me too, but I was too fast for him." My mind raced, trying to figure out the connection between Dimmitt and Garrett.

Garrett's sneer grew wider. "He was my half-brother.

No one kills a Dimmitt or Garrett without family taking out their pound of flesh."

"And so that's why you lied?"

The smug gleam in his eyes was all the answer I needed.

That night after I tied him up like a thrown calf, I left him with a chilling promise. "You'll tell the truth. That, I promise you."

Hugh Garrett glared at me then spat on the ground. "There's my answer."

The morning of the second day, Red Eagle met up with us. After leaving Nat and the freed captives with the Army at Fort Kimble, he had immediately headed back.

He eyed Garrett coldly. "This the one?"

I nodded.

"What he say?"

"Nothing. Not yet. Says he won't talk."

A leering grin played over Red Eagle's face. He laid his hand on the butt of his knife. "Men always speak. If not soon, then later. But they always speak."

Garrett's Adam's apple bobbed up and down several times but he remained silent.

We were another day from the Llano. From a sky that looked like a white bowl, the sun baked the earth. From time to time throughout the long day, I glanced over my shoulder, half expecting to see a cloud of dust.

To my surprise, we reached the ruined cabin without spotting any evidence of pursuit.

"Let's go to the cave for tonight. In the morning, I'll ride in for the captain."

At the cave, I dismounted and pulled Garrett from the saddle and shoved him inside. Red Eagle took our ponies and led them deeper into the canyon to the hidden corral.

After a supper of coffee and jerky broth that night, the first hot food my belly had welcomed in over a week, I tied Garrett good and snug.

Red Eagle pulled out his wicked knife and spent the remainder of the evening sharpening it and grinning wickedly at Garrett.

From time to time that evening, I thought I saw something in Garrett's eyes, something besides fear, but I shrugged it off.

Next morning, I rode in for Captain Irwin.

When we returned two hours later, I found Red Eagle sprawled on the cavern floor, the back of his head crushed. Beside him lay a sharp block of granite covered with blood.

Muttering a curse, I hurried to the corral, but all three animals were still there. I looked around the canyon, trying to calm the rage burning in my chest. Garrett must have struck Red Eagle only minutes earlier. Otherwise, he would have found the ponies.

He's on foot, and I knew with cold satisfaction I could track any man—white or Indian—on foot.

Red Eagle's Spencer carbine and gun belt were missing. I strung his bow and sheath of arrows over my shoulder then grabbed my Yellowboy Henry.

I paused in the mouth of the cave. "Captain, I'd appreciate it if you'd send Nat back out here to look after Red Eagle."

Captain Irwin nodded. "I'll do that." He paused. "I regret I was suspicious of him. Certainly, the families of those captives he brought in will never forget him."

For a moment, my emotions clouded my eyes. I nodded. "He was a brave man. The two feathers he wears tells his story."

Irwin frowned. "I don't understand."

"See the one dark at the top with two plumes at the tip?"

"I see it."

"That means he was first to strike an enemy. And the second one, the solid black one split up the middle, it means he has received many wounds." I nodded slowly. "Yes, Captain. My brother was a brave warrior." I looked up into his eyes. "And I plan to avenge him."

Garrett was easy to follow. He had left the cave running. Stones were overturned, their damp bellies grinning at the sun; branches were snapped, dangling at the ground; and at places, his boot heels had dug deeply into the soft soil.

After a few hundred yards heading out of the canyon, his trail turned back. I frowned, then realized he had spotted us riding in, so he had no choice but to go deeper in the canyon.

Ten minutes later I spotted him, scrabbling up a trail on one wall of the box canyon about a quarter of a mile ahead of me. I might have hit him with a lead plum from the Henry at this distance but it would have involved more luck than I wanted to chance. Besides, I needed him alive.

I didn't figure he had spotted me yet, so I started up a chimney in the canyon wall knowing he couldn't see me. The only trouble was I couldn't climb as fast as he could.

Sweat soaked my clothes as I strained to shinny up the chimney with my back against one wall and my feet against the other. Halfway up, my Colt slipped from my holster. I had forgotten to fit the rawhide loop about the hammer. I muttered a soft curse and continued climbing. I still had my Yellowboy Henry.

Finally, I reached the rim. I peered over the edge, seeing no sign of Garrett. Taking a deep breath, I heaved my exhausted body over the rim.

I struggled to my feet, and suddenly, a powerful blow followed by the boom of a Spencer ripped the Henry from my grip, numbing my fingers. I threw myself behind an oak.

Garrett's smug voice carried across the rim. "Things look different now, huh, Thornton? Thought you was smart, huh? You ain't smart. Neither was that Injun."

"I should have figured you being the kind of vermin to jump a body from behind."

He laughed. "He should have been paying attention."

I looked around, searching for a way out. Across a small clearing, I saw a narrow passage between a jumble of boulders. I hoped it wasn't a dead end. Taking a deep breath, I bolted across the clearing and leaped into the passage just as a slug from the .58 caliber Spencer knocked a chunk out of the limestone rock.

My wounded leg buckled on me, and I sprawled on the rock. Fresh blood stained my trousers. Limping, I hurried down the passage that twisted and turned like a rabbit warren. Behind me, I heard Garrett clambering down the trail. Suddenly, I jerked to a halt. The main passage continued forward, but a secondary one cut a few feet to the right, then several feet back around another corner.

Cold determination settled over me.

Slipping the bow from around my shoulder and nocking an arrow, I slipped back into the secondary passage and waited. If he followed me back here I'd be ready.

If not, then I would become the stalker.

Moments later, I heard the thud of his boot heels on rocks and the jangle of his spurs as he hurried up the trail, bypassing the narrow passage in which I had hidden.

Quickly, I stepped into the main trail and drew the

bow, aiming at his back. "Hold it right there, Garrett. Don't move a muscle."

He froze. "All you got is that bow, Thornton. I ain't blind. I saw you didn't have no sidearm."

"I can't argue with you there, Garrett, but this yard-long arrow will kill a jasper as certain as a two hundred grain slug. Now, drop that Spencer."

I had the arrow drawn back to my jawbone. The braided rawhide string was stretched so tight it vibrated. My weary muscles were beginning to give in to the strain of holding the powerful bow at the ready.

Still not moving, he laughed. "Kill me and the Army will never know the truth."

"Then I'll have to live with that."

"You shouldn't have killed my brother."

"He shouldn't have murdered the old man and tried to kill me."

"Maybe not, but I ruined your life like you ruined my family's."

A familiar voice broke the silence. "An eye for eye. Is that what you'd say, Mr. Garrett?"

We both looked up to see Captain Irwin step from behind a cedar on the granite ledge several feet above our heads. He held his Army issue revolver on Garrett.

With a scream of rage, Garrett spun and fired. At the same time I released my arrow, and above my head the captain's revolver roared.

Shards of granite dug into my flesh and stung my cheeks. I closed my eyes and spun away. When I looked back around, Garrett lay on the ground in a spreading pool of blood.

"You all right, Thornton?" Captain Irwin called out.

I knelt by Garrett. My arrow had penetrated his heart, and the captain's slug had caught him between the eyes. He was dead. I nodded. "Yeah. I'm all right."

"I figured I'd best follow you."

I chuckled. "I'm mighty glad you did, Captain."

Later in his office at the fort with Nat looking on, Captain Irwin nodded to Lucy Coulter. "Mrs. Coulter told me why you were after Garrett. I heard enough up on the canyon rim to convince me he lied." He paused and frowned. "The war's over; the Confederate Army has been surrendered and disbanded; the Confederacy no longer exists. I don't know if we can ever officially clear your name, but as for me and those who were with me at Brown's Ferry, you will never be considered a coward or traitor." He smiled sadly. "That might be the best we can do, Thornton."

I nodded. "Reckon that'll have to be enough, Captain." I smiled at Lucy and Nat. "First thing in the morning, I figure we need to ride out to the ranch and get started rebuilding. We got a heap of work to do."

Nat grinned. "Yes, sir."

Lucy's eyes glowed.

That night, I lay on my blanket outside the enlisted men's quarters and stared at the stars overhead. As soon as the ranch was up and running, I'd ride out to Santa Fe and see Damita and her father. Then I'd return to the Llano River Valley and ask Lucy to be my wife.

1	16
2	17
3	18
4	19
5	20
6	21
7	22
8	23
9	24
10	25
11	26
12	27
13	28
14	29
15	30
1S	4S
2S	5S
3S	6S